A God Among Men

Endless Storm

Kyle Hodge

A God Among Men

Endless Storm

By Kyle Hodge

Kyle Hodge

AGodAmongMenSeries@gmail.com
Facebook.com/AGodAmongMenSeries

ISBN: 979-8-9876483-0-8 (Paperback)
ISBN: 979-8-9876483-1-5 (E-Book)

Any references to historical events, real people, or real places are used fictitiously. Names, characters, and places are products of the author's imagination.

First printing edition 2023.
Printed in the United States of America

About The Author

Kyle Hodge is a first-time writer who wants to bring his thoughts and creativity to life. *"Endless Storm"* is the beginning of, hopefully, many stories he wants to tell.

Kyle currently resides in Pennsylvania with his beautiful wife. He is also the proud father of an amazing little boy with a second one on the way.

Kyle is currently working on the second installment in the *"A God Among Men"* series.

In memory of
Tim S Hodge

A God Among Men

To my beautiful wife – Thank you for all the support you have given me since the beginning. Thank you for supporting Austin Kale's adventure. I love you so much.

To my boys – Time is flying by. Both of you bring so much joy into my life. I can't not wait to see you two playing and laughing with each other. Daddy loves you both very much.

Mom – You have always been my biggest supporter since the day I was born. Thank you for always believing in me and helping me become the best man I can be. I love you.

Dad – I miss you more than anything. I know you would have loved this story. I know you are looking down on me and smiling. I love you.

Kyle Hodge

Table Of Contents

Kyle Hodge

Chapter 1
Beginning

Long ago, before time began, a brother and sister were alone in the universe. They were nameless Gods, just existing in the emptiness of space. They never got along or agreed on anything. Finally, the brother God decided it was time for a change. He used his powers to create various worlds. There was just one problem. The planets were dying. Each one failed faster than the next. As each world died, the sister God could feel herself growing stronger. In the next world he created, he added water to balance out the land and creatures to swim and explore the watery depths. He made mountains to touch the clouds and creatures that could walk and roam the land. He added trees and bushes for the animals to eat from and to survive. He called it: Earth.

The sister God didn't feel any stronger when this new world was created. She saw that the planet called Earth was thriving and very much alive. This angered the sister God. She wanted more power. She was cunning. She talked to her brother and expressed how tired he looked after creating all those worlds. She suggested that it was a lot for them to take care of themselves, so she helped him to create other Gods to rule over different aspects of the world. Everything seemed right in the world, but the brother God thought it was missing something. He added one more creature to the world, little naked creatures. They were called humans. They were different sizes, shapes, and colors. The Gods and humans lived in harmony. The humans worshiped the Gods. They made shrines for them and prayed to them. The Gods provided anything they needed.

That is until some of the humans began to rebel. The Gods did not like that, and they were very angry. They punished the world. The brother God did not want that. He decided to do what none of the other Gods had ever done. He fell to Earth. He helped defend Earth against the other Gods' wrath.

The sister God had her followers and worshipers on Earth, but when they stopped worshiping, she wasn't receiving the amount of power she wanted. She allowed the other Gods to punish the world even though her brother was on Earth defending them. She decided that if he wanted to defend the humans and the Earth, then he could stay there. She banished him from living among the Gods.

Over time humans populated the world, and as time went on, the human mind developed quickly, and amazing technological advances were made. Humans started believing they didn't need the Gods anymore. Gods made mountains, but humans made skyscrapers just as tall. Humans made machines to explore the ocean just like the fish the Gods created. Gods created birds to fly high in the sky. Humans made giant metal birds that fly higher. The humans no longer needed to ask the Gods to cure the sick or punish the wicked. They had doctors and medicine to heal the sick, and they had their laws and justice system put into place. Man no longer needed Gods.

Shrines we're forgotten. Prayers were said less and less each day. The sister God was not happy about this at all. The Gods then went and showed their power to the humans. Deadly hurricanes destroyed the towns. Blizzards crippled the biggest cities. Tsunamis and earthquakes left behind complete destruction. Hundreds of thousands of years passed, and the Gods were still trying to scare the humans into worshiping them. Although the progress had been slow, each year, more and more humans were praying again, but out of fear, not love.

No other God wanted to take human form to walk the Earth. They used their powers from afar. They never wanted to stoop down and join the humans. Until one God swallowed his pride and went to tell the sister God that he was willing to go to Earth to remind the humans that Gods were still in control. The sister God wanted the humans to be put in their place. She agreed, and the God took his human form and fell to Earth.

As time went on, the brother God took more of a step back and kept who he was a secret from humans. For the most part, he took the form of a beautiful raven. He flew the skies and kept an eye on the humans, helping wherever he was able. He heard of another God coming to Earth and knew it couldn't be good. He knew he had to put a stop to his sister's plans.

The brother God had been watching one family very closely. The Kale family. Brian Kale and Leah Kale. They live at 128 Winter Crest Lane in a town called Silverdale in Florida. Brian was a construction worker with short brown hair and brown eyes. He served in the military as a pilot before he was married. He loves the town and had helped build a few of the buildings there. He is usually the first person to volunteer if someone needs help. Leah works at the Silverdale hospital and had long blonde hair and brown eyes. She was always cooking or baking something for her friends and family and sometimes for town activities. They have been trying for the past two years to have a baby but were unaware that Brian was unable to have children. The brother God kept an eye on the Kale family by sitting on top of the house across the street as a raven.

One night, he saw Brian come home drunk and smelling of whisky. The brother God flew down next to Brian's truck and finally took his human form again after hundreds of years. Brian started to get out of the truck. He was drunk and stumbling. He dropped his keys as he got out. He reached down for them, and once he stood back up, he saw a man grab his shoulder, and he blacked out. He was laid down in his truck, and the brother God went into the house. Leah was already sound asleep. The brother God walked to the side of the bed. He closed his eyes for a moment. When he opened his eyes, they were glowing white. He put his hand over his heart and slowly pulled his hand away. There was a small white light floating over his hand. He pulled the light out of his own heart. The light had a tiny little pulse. He put his hand down in front of Leah's stomach, and the light floated into her stomach. Her stomach lit up for a second and went back to normal. The brother God's eyes went back to normal as well. He turned and walked back outside. He put another hand on Brian, and he was no longer drunk or smelled like whisky. The brother God also cured him of not being able to have children. He carried Brian inside and put him in bed like nothing ever happened. The brother God went back outside, took raven form, and flew away.

Every night since then, he sat and watched over them from across the street. Two weeks later, it seemed as though Leah wasn't feeling her best. She would be seen running to and from the bathroom. Seeing negative pregnancy tests after negative pregnancy tests. The thought of taking another one made her upset. She decided it was necessary to rule out the possibility, but this time, it was positive. That little glowing light was a child that the brother God formed from his own heart and soul.

A few months later, Leah had a baby bump. She was sitting on the couch after a long day at the hospital. She was watching the news and couldn't believe what she was seeing or hearing. A man was walking down the road with his arms out wide in the middle of a hurricane. The news camera zoomed in on the man.

"Honey, there's this weird-looking man just walking in that bad hurricane overseas. It's almost like he's enjoying it." Leah said to Brian.

"The world is full of weirdos," Brian replied as he was cleaning the dishes from dinner.

"No, I mean, he looks really strange." Leah described the man as a six-and-a-half to seven-foot tall, very muscular-looking viking. One side of his head was shaved, and the other was adorned with a tattoo of a lightning bolt. The rest of his hair was golden blonde, with blue tints braided down over his left shoulder. Three black lines of what looked like war paint go from his forehead over his left eye down to his chin. The weirdest feature were his eyes. They were glowing blue, like something you would see in a comic.

"You're joking, right?" As Brian walked into the living room to look at the TV. He was surprised. He couldn't believe it either. "You sure this isn't a movie you're watching?"

"Positive!" she looked down, rubbing her belly. "I want our baby to be safe," she said in a sad voice. "There are so many scary things in the world." Leah had a tear roll down her face from the thought of something bad happening to her baby.

Brian grabbed a clean towel and wiped the tear away. "I can't quite put my finger on it, but something tells me we will be okay." He hugged Leah and looked out the window and saw the raven. This gave him peace and he made a little smile. As if all the worry in the world left his body. "We will be okay."

The news reporter screamed and ran away, and the camera operator dropped the camera as he ran with her. The camera landed, still pointing at the strange-looking man. Brian and Leah turn back to look at the TV. The man on the TV was spinning one of his arms in a circle above his head, and the wind picked up. He put his other hand in the air and threw it down. Lightning struck the ground right in front of him. He turned around and saw police cars driving toward him.

"You humans need to learn your place in the universe." said the man with a deep raspy voice. The man lunged his arms forward, and lightning shot out from his hands and struck the police cars, causing them to explode. He turned back to look toward the camera. "I am a God, and you will all bow and worship me!" He said with such anger as the lighting was striking all around him. He walked up to the camera and picked it up.

A God Among Men

"I am The Storm. And you haven't seen anything yet." The news feed was cut off right after that.

Leah looked right at Brian. "What are we going to do? That man said he was a God and that humans need to learn their place in the universe. What does that mean? What if he comes here?" She sounded terrified.

"I never heard of a God on Earth. I always thought they lived in the clouds or something. There must be a reason why he is on Earth now. I'm sure he's not even going to worry about a small town like Silverdale. We will cross that bridge if we get to it. You have nothing to worry about." Brian said as he turned back to the kitchen to finish the dishes. Little did they know their lives and their baby's life were about to change forever.

Chapter 2
Back To School

Seventeen years have gone by. The Kale Family had almost tripled in size since that night they were watching the news. Brian and Leah are proud parents of seventeen-year-old Austin Kale, who had brown hair and brown eyes, just like his dad. His fourteen-year-old little sister Elizabeth Kale, who had long blond hair just like her mom, and a one-year-old little girl, named Ava. Summer had just ended, and the first day of school was tomorrow. Austin was going into his senior year at Silverdale High School. Elizabeth, or Elsie as her family and friends call her, was now a freshman at the school.

Austin was not the most popular kid in school. He doesn't play any sports, but he attends all sporting events. He doesn't talk to anyone at school other than his best friend, Marcus, with whom he shares a love for video games and superhero movies. Austin and Marcus have been best friends ever since Marcus moved to Silverdale when he was about five years old. They went to the same karate class throughout elementary school, and they attended the same summer camp every year until middle school started. They live down the road from each other, and both work at the local ice cream shop during the summer.

Marcus moved here to Silverdale because his parents got jobs here, but they aren't around much. Marcus was the star running back for the Silverdale Knights, the high school football team, and was one of the top students in the school with grades. Unlike Austin, Marcus was one of the more popular kids at school.

Austin's favorite teacher was Mr. Davidson, the history teacher at the high school. Austin had always done well in his class. He always sits in the front row, closest to Mr. Davidson's desk.

Now we can't forget about Olivia. She had medium black hair and blue eyes. Olivia was a new student during Austin's freshman year. They had some of the same classes. Austin likes her but was too nervous to tell her, or even talk to her, for that matter. She loved it when he got nervous around her.

For the most part, Austin was pretty much forgotten at school. Other students didn't know his name. He kept his head down and did his work. He had a simple life.

The first week of school was almost over. Austin and Marcus were walking to work Thursday afternoon after school let out. They only had a few shifts left now that school had started up again. They always walk the same sidewalk every time they go to work. Today was just a little bit different.

They heard a man yell and glass break. Austin and Marcus ran around the corner and saw a man on the ground and three other men around him kicking him and trying to rob him. Austin and Marcus hurried and ran to help him. Marcus tackled one of them to the ground. Austin threw his school bag at the second man, which caught him off guard and staggered him. Austin then tackled the third man. The second one threw Austin's bag off of him and grabbed Austin around his neck. Marcus came and punched the man in the side of the head, making him let go of Austin. Austin and Marcus stood side by side with their fists up. The three thugs stood across from them. One of the thugs stepped forward and threw a punch. Austin ducked and dodged it and threw a punch of his own. Austin didn't touch the thug. When he threw his punch, a strong gust of wind came and knocked the thug backward hard. The wind seemed only to follow Austin's fist. The wind didn't touch anyone else. Austin looked down at his fist. The other two looked at each other and picked the third man up and ran away.

"That was some wind," Marcus said.

The thugs were stumbling as they ran down the road. Austin turned to help the man up. Grabbing him by the arm and one hand on his back, he was able to get the man back to his feet. The man was about six feet tall and about fifty to sixty years old. He seemed to be in great shape for his age.

"Are you okay, mister?" Marcus asked as Austin noticed a tattoo on the older man's arm.

"Yes, I am, thank you both," he said.

"Is that a raven?" Austin asked quickly.

"Why yes, it is, young man. You know your birds?" The man asked as he and Marcus picked up his bags.

"No, just ravens. My mom and dad are kind of obsessed with them."

A God Among Men

Austin and Marcus helped the man get all his bags into his house. Two of the bags had broken jars in them from falling to the ground.

"You know, in ancient history, ravens are said to be the wise, all-knowing messenger. The bridge between our world and worlds beyond. A bird of protection". The man told Austin and Marcus as he started unpacking his bags. Austin and Marcus just looked at each other from across the kitchen, both thinking the man was crazy.

"But then again. Sometimes they are just birds." the man said with a little chuckle. "It depends if you believe stuff like that."

The man was looking around the house. "How can I ever repay you boys for helping me?"

"There's no need, sir. We are just glad you are okay," Marcus said. Marcus started to walk to the front door. "Austin, we have to get to work."

The man walked over to a bookshelf. He grabbed a gold coin off the top, walked over to Austin, and set the coin in his hand. He spoke quietly enough for Marcus not to hear.

"This is a very special coin. If you are ever in danger or lost or in any trouble, flip the coin and help will come." The man looked Austin directly in his eyes. He nodded his head and patted him on the shoulder.

"Shouldn't you boys be off to work?" the man said.

Austin was staring at the man like he was crazy.

"Austin, we're going to be late! Let's go!" Marcus yelled, as he ran out the front door. Austin snapped out of it. He grabbed his bag and ran out of the door after Marcus. The man walked out to the front porch waving to Austin and Marcus. Austin was able to catch up to Marcus. He looked back at the man's house and swore he saw a raven fly away from the front porch.

A few hours passed and Austin and Marcus were in the middle of their shift at the ice cream shop. "That man was a little weird, wasn't he?" Marcus said, laughing. "What was all the talk about ravens?"

"I'm not sure, but something about him seemed familiar." Austin said, looking at the coin the man gave him.

"What did he say to you when he gave you that?" Marcus pointed at the coin.

"Some mumbo jumbo stuff like that stuff about the raven" Austin put the coin in his pocket and stood up to help the customer that just walked in.

Austin stayed up for a long time that night just looking at the coin. Something seemed familiar about that man, like he knew him from somewhere. It took him a long time to fall asleep, but eventually, he did.

The next morning, Austin and Marcus walked to school with Elsie. Once they got to school, Elsie ran to meet up with her friends. Everyone seemed to be staring at Austin and Marcus.

Elsie ran back to her big brother. "You're in a video that everyone is watching. You saved that old man."

"He was getting attacked. I had to help him." Austin said as he and Marcus followed her to her friends to watch the video.

"We needed to help him and get him in his home. He lives right on the corner of Grey Stone Road."

"Wait, that red brick house?" Elsie asked.

"Yeah, that's the one. Really nice house. I didn't know anyone lived there." Austin said, looking at Marcus. He nodded in agreement.

A God Among Men

"That's because no one does." Elsie laughed. "That house has been abandoned ever since we were born. It's all damaged inside."

Austin looked at Marcus. Both of them were very confused.

"I didn't know you could fight," Olivia said as she walked up to Austin, pretending to punch his shoulder.

"I... I. Can't. I just... he was..." Austin was stumbling with his words. Olivia smiled and walked to class.

"Smooth," Marcus said, putting his arm around him.

"Shut up," Austin replied, lightly jabbing Marcus in the ribs and walked to class.

Chapter 3
The First Men

The bell rang, and everyone hurried into their seats. Austin walked past the teacher's desk to find his. He sat his backpack on the tile floor next to his desk and pulled out a green notebook and his history book. He glanced up at the white board and saw three words written on it.

The First Men

"Can you all take your seats, please?" asked Mr. Davidson. "I hope you all had a good night and completed your homework." All the students pulled out their homework as Mr. Davidson walked by to collect it. "Can I have your homework, Austin?" he asked as he approached the desk.

Silence

"Austin?"

"I don't have it, Mr. Davidson," Austin said, looking out the window.

A God Among Men

"Is everything alright? That's not like you." Mr. Davidson said, leaning down toward Austin.

"Just had a lot on my mind last night. I'm sorry," Austin said.

"If you ever need to talk, I'm here," Mr. Davidson said.

Austin just nodded back.

"Okay, class, as you can tell from the board, today we will be learning about the First Men. As you all know, everything was created by the two nameless Gods. The world, stars, us, and even other Gods. But does anyone know why they are nameless?" he asked the class. No one knew the answer.

"They are nameless because they weren't created. They were just there. They never needed to have names. They created the first humans. They called them the First Men. Does anyone know where?" Mr. Davidson asked.

He saw a few students raise their hands. Everyone else was taking notes. Answers like Greece, Russia, the US, and England were shouted out but were all wrong.

"All are great guesses, but there is one correct answer. Egypt. Long ago, humans had connections with the Gods. They needed something to call them. The First Men gave them names." Mr. Davidson looked at the class and saw they were all confused. He began to draw a circle on the board. "Everything doesn't have a name until someone names it. The First Men were the ones to give the Gods names" he continued to draw a curved line with two smaller circles inside the big circle. "They were referred to by many names. Light and Dark, Life and Death, Good and Evil" he turned back toward class "Yin and Yang."

"One God cannot exist without the other. The God of light and the Goddess of Dark, forever trapped in an eternal dance. Circling each other for all time." He continued, "The First Men worshiped the Gods. They built shrines for them. Today they are known as the great pyramids." Mr. Davison said as he walked over and sat on top of his desk.

"I thought the pyramids were tombs for the pharaohs?" One girl called out in class.

"That is correct. That brings us to the fall of the First Men. You see, the Gods provided anything the First Men needed. Everything was peaceful. No sickness, no war, and no one went hungry. The First Men didn't worry about anything. They were able to live for hundreds of years. Eventually, the First Men started to feel like "Gods" themselves. They took everything for granted. Their long lives, never getting sick, and being able to build great shrines for the Gods without the Gods' help. They started thinking they didn't need the Gods anymore. This led to the rebellion. The First Men rebelled against the Gods. They stopped praying and stopped worshiping. They used the shrines as tombs for their loved ones or the pharaohs. This did not make the Gods happy. The rebellion caused the Gods to show their true power. The Earth started to shake, mountains broke apart as fire came from the ground, storms of wind and water formed, and land began to freeze. Many lives were lost during the rebellion," Mr. Davidson said sadly as he walked around his desk to sit in his seat. "Now we are punished for what the First Men did."

The class started to look worried.

"But that's just life. Everything we do today will affect the lives of tomorrow," Mr. Davidson said, trying to be positive for the class.

"Don't let the people of tomorrow be punished for what we do today. Be better than the First Men. There's no changing what happened. We will never be back to how it was before, but we can make it better."

Austin raised his hand.

"You have a question, Austin?" Asked Mr. Davidson.

"What if the Gods didn't exist?" Austin asked.

"I do not have an answer for that, but maybe the world would know peace once again. Or maybe it would fall apart. No one knows." Mr. Davidson said as he handed out the homework.

"What happened to the First Men after the rebellion?" asked one of the other girls in class.

"It's not in the schoolbooks, but it's rumored that the God of light, Yin, fought off the other Gods. He defended the humans. Eventually, he convinced the other Gods to stop the destructions they were causing and punish the men without killing them. His sister, Yang, decided to respect her brother's wishes. She caused the rest of the First Men to be unable to communicate. They were able to speak but did not understand each other. They spoke different languages. They were also banished to all corners of the world. That's how humans populated the entire world. They were driven away from Egypt."

The bell rang to let the students know the class was over and time for lunch. None of the students moved a muscle. Mr. Davidson started to clean the board for his next class after lunch. He continued to talk to the class.

"The God of light was the only God who helped the humans. They were his creation, and he did not want to see what he created to be destroyed. The God of light took the form of a raven and went to Earth watching over his creation."

This got the attention of Austin, who was drawing in his notebook as the teacher was talking.

"There was a man named Aggon. He and his family always prayed to the God of light. He taught his family to be thankful for what was given to them and to help anyone else in need. They thanked Yin for breathing life into them and for always providing for them. Yin would always sit on a rooftop across from Aggon's house to watch over Aggon and his family."

Austin turned pale. Almost like he had seen a ghost. He keeps thinking of the raven that always sits on the house across the street from his.

"There's no way," he mumbled to himself.

"What was that, Austin?" asked Mr. Davidson.

"Oh, nothing," he said anxiously. "What happened after that?"

"Well, when the God of light heard of the punishment coming, he flew to Aggon's home. Aggon was outside his house working when he saw the raven land on a tree branch right in front of him. He and the raven were staring at each other. The raven flew right toward Aggon, landing on the ground in front of him. Once the raven landed, a cloud of white smoke appeared. Yin was standing there. He told Aggon to pack his bags, get his family, and follow him. He did just as he was told. Yin led Aggon and his family to a cave far away. He was providing for them and keeping them safe. Inside the cave, Yin spoke to Aggon once more, telling him, he needs to be able to protect his family if any of the Gods come looking for them. Yin transformed back into the raven and flew away. A large feather fell from the raven and landed on the ground in front of Aggon's feet. The feather hardened and formed a blade. The Sword of Aggon." Mr. Davidson was telling the class.

"How do you know all this if it's not in the book?" Marcus asked.

"Well, before I became a teacher, my great-grandfather used to travel the world. He wanted to explore anything and everything. In his travels, he came across a very old library full of scrolls and other things. He said that once inside, he came across an old box with a raven insignia on the top. Inside was a scroll written by Aggon himself. He left the library with plans to go back. But sadly, no one has been able to find the library again. I assume it was destroyed. It's a shame, really, all that history and knowledge lost."

The class was amazed by it.

"What happened to Aggon and his family?" one of the other boys asked.

"No one knows. That's where the scroll ends. As far as I know, that was the last scroll of Aggon."

"There are other scrolls? Where are they?" Marcus called out.

"Maybe in a museum somewhere or lost forever or destroyed." Mr. Davidson was packing up and preparing for the next class. "Enough for today. Off you go. Lunch will be over soon."

The students got up and started to walk out of the classroom. Each one talked about the story Mr. Davidson had just finished teaching them. Marcus was about to walk out of the class when he saw Austin still sitting at his desk, staring out the window. He walked over and nudged him on the shoulder.

"Dude, you okay?" Marcus asked.

"What?" Austin replied with a tremble in his voice, "Oh yeah, I'm fine. I uhh... I just zoned out, that's all." Austin couldn't dare tell Marcus that he thinks a raven was stalking his family just like Aggon's. He was afraid he would be made fun of.

"I'll meet you at lunch. I have to run to my locker." Austin said.

Everyone was able to make it to the second half of lunch in time. Austin found where Marcus and Olivia were sitting in the lunchroom and went and sat with them. He pulled out his brown paper bag. He was still thinking of the story and how it must be just a weird coincidence that a raven sits on the house across the street also. He starts to open his bag.

"BOO!" Austin jumped like his soul left his body. He turned around to see his little sister standing behind him.

"Did I get you?" she asked as she started to laugh. Marcus and Olivia were holding back their laughter.

"What do you want, Elsie?" he said seemingly annoyed. He was embarrassed that she had scared him in front of Olivia.

"Mom mixed up our lunches." She held out a brown bag with his name on it. He looked down and saw her name on the bag he had. He swapped the bags and turned to his friends.

"You handled that well," Marcus said, still holding back the laughter.

"Oh, stop," Olivia said as she reached over and grabbed Austin's hand. "He just had a lot on his mind and was caught off guard." Austin began to blush. "It's not every day you beat up some thugs and then get scared by a 14-year-old girl all in 24 hours," she said as she started to laugh too.

Austin hid his face in his arms on the table. He was feeling really embarrassed.

"I'm kidding, Austin. I'm sorry," Olivia said, "hurry up. Next class is starting soon."

Throughout the rest of the school day, Austin would get distracted very often. His mind would wonder, and he swore he kept seeing a raven outside the school flying around. Before he knew it, the final bell rang, and all the students were leaving to go home. Austin met up with Elsie and Marcus and walked home. Marcus lived a few houses down from the Kales. He would always come to say good morning to Mr. and Mrs. Kale before the kids walked to school and would also say have a great evening after they got back from school. Today when they got home, they walked inside, and Mr. and Mrs. Kale were waiting for them. They did not look happy.

"I'm just going to go," Marcus whispered to Austin. "Have a good night, Mr. and Mrs. Kale," he said as he left the house, shutting the door behind him.

"Is there something you want to tell us, Austin?" their mom asked with her arms crossed.

"Is Austin in trouble? Can I stay and watch?" Elsie asked.

"Go to your room, Elsie." their dad said with a strict tone in his voice.

"But please, I want to..."

"Now, Elizabeth." he demanded, interrupting her. Their parents only used her full name when it was serious. She walked back to her room and closed the door behind her.

"Start talking." Austin's dad said to Austin as he pulled out a kitchen chair for him to sit on.

"I'm not sure what's going on," Austin said with a very confused look on his face.

His mom pulled up the video on social media of Austin fighting. "First, when did this happen? Why didn't you tell us? And when is this ever okay? And on top of that, your school called, and you haven't handed in any of your homework today, and you didn't participate today at all. What is going on?" she asked.

"Okay, well, you see, the fight, I was trying to... He needed help. He was getting attacked. And school, I was in class, and I didn't..."

Knock knock knock

Austin didn't know what to say or how to explain it. He was fumbling with his words because he had never really made his parents mad before. Austin let out a big breath when someone knocked on the door. That happened at the right moment.

Austin's dad went to open the door. "Can I help you, sir?"

Mrs. Kale and Austin got up to see who it was. The man that Austin and Marcus saved was standing at the door.

Chapter 4
The Storm

"H-Hello, mister. Is everything okay?" Austin asked as he was confused about how the man knew he lived here.

"You know this man?" his mom asked.

"This was the man Marcus and I helped in that video."

"This young man was so helpful the other day." he said.

"I saw you and your friend walk here just a little bit ago and was wondering if you could help me with my bags again." The older man said as he looked back to Austin. Austin looked at his dad, and his dad nodded.

As Austin followed the older man back to his house, Austin got curious. "Why did those men start robbing you? You look like you could have taken them."

"I let them." the man said with no hesitation.

"Wait." Austin stopped walking. "You let them attack you?" Austin asked in surprise.

"Yes, I let them rob me and attack me. I knew you were about to walk around the corner, and I just had to make sure you were ready."

Austin grabbed the man's shoulder and spun him so they were facing each other. "What do you mean to make sure I'm ready? Ready for what? How did you know I was about to walk around the corner?"

The man just pointed inside the house. "I'll show you." The man turned and walked inside the house.

Austin hesitated. He looked back down the street toward the corner. He was thinking about running back home.

"Don't you want to know who you really are?" the man yelled from the doorway.

Austin looked back to the man's house. He took a deep breath as he started to walk to the house. He walked up the steps and into the front door. Once inside, the front door slammed shut. Scared, he turned back and looked at the door. He tried opening the door, but it would not budge. He turned back to look around the house. Only he wasn't in the house anymore. It looked like he was in a very old, ancient building full of giant statues. He refused to take one more step. The man walked out from behind a pillar.

"Is this some kind of trick?!" Austin yelled out in fear. "Who are you? What do you want from me?"

"Never mind that." the man said back to him. "Do you know who you are?" he asked.

"I'm ... Austin Kale." he said as he was looking around.

"Yes... and no." the man said back to him. "That is your name, but not who you are... well, not who you are meant to be."

"What's that supposed to mean?" Austin asked.

"Do you know where we are standing right now?" the man asked.

A God Among Men

"I don't know, some old building? I must be dreaming." Austin answered.

"This is no dream. We're standing in the temple of the Gods. It was built by the First Men."

"Temple of the Gods..." Austin said back to himself softly as he continued to look around. "Why haven't I heard if this place before?" Austin asked the older man.

"Because it was destroyed long ago," the man replied. "This is what the temple use to look like."

"So... are you a God?" Austin asked.

"I am, to some. Not everyone believes in Gods anymore."

"Okay, okay." Austin was starting to breathe heavily, not really believing what he was hearing. He closed his eyes tight. "This isn't real," he whispered over and over to himself. He opened one eye slowly, and the man was still standing there.

"Did it work?" the man asked Austin.

Austin sighed. "Okay, well, if you're a God, then which one are you?"

"That's not important right now." the man said as he walked up to Austin. "What is important, is him." the man looked up and pointed behind Austin. Austin turned around and began to look up. There was a big statue of a man.

"I've seen him before, on the news. I think I learned about him in school too. He's a God like you, right?" Austin asked.

"That's The Storm. Yes, he's a God, and he's also on Earth right now, causing chaos and destruction."

"Okay? He looks scary, but what does that have to do with me?" Austin asked as he turned back to the man.

"Because you need to stop him." the man said.

"Me?!" Austin asked surprisingly. "How am I going to stop that?!" pointing back to the statue. "That is a God. A powerful and scary God. And I'm... "

"A God," the man said, interrupting Austin.

"No, no, absolutely not. You're insane," Austin said, pointing at the man.

"There is a whole world out there. Full of people just like the man who fell and was getting attacked. The man that YOU saved," the man said firmly, putting his finger on Austin's chest. "The other Gods are attacking the people of this world, and you can help them."

Austin shook his head no. "You're wrong. I'm not who or what you think I am." Austin swiped the man's hand away. He turned and started to head out the door.

"You can't run from this. When you change your mind, I'll still be here!" the man yelled as Austin walked away toward his house.

Austin couldn't believe what he saw or what he heard. "I hope I'm dreaming," he said to himself as he approached his house. He was hoping that he would wake up any minute. He walked in the front door to his dad was standing there.

"Everything okay?" his dad asked.

He couldn't even try to explain what had just happened. They wouldn't believe him. He thought he would get in more trouble if they thought he was lying.

"Yeah, just a few bags he needed help with," Austin said.

"That's very nice that you helped him again." his dad said as he patted him on the back.

"Promise me you'll pay attention in school, okay? I don't want to get another phone call. You've been doing so well, and it's your last year before college." his dad said.

"I know, I know, yes, I promise," Austin said, as he walked back to his room. "It's been a long day. I'm going to bed early. Good night, love you," as he closed the door.

"Love you, see you in the morning," both his dad and mom said.

Austin laid in bed, trying to fall asleep, but his mind just kept racing. He grabbed his phone off the nightstand and searched *The Storm* on the internet. The first thing to pop up was a picture of the man who looked just like the statue he saw. He scrolled down more and saw an article talking about an endless storm that had formed over Norway. It's been storming there for the past seventeen years since the day the God fell to Earth.

"This is ridiculous." he thought to himself. He put his phone down, rolled over and was finally able to fall asleep. The next day was a normal day. He woke up, got ready for school, and ate breakfast.

Marcus walked into the house. "Good morning, Kale family!"

The whole family said good morning back. Marcus walked up to Ava, who was sitting in her highchair.

"You are getting so big. I can't wait to tell you all about your weirdo big brother."

"She's going to learn you're the weirdo first," Austin said as he smacked Marcus's chest as he walked by. "Time to go," he added.

Austin, Marcus, and Elsie all grabbed their book bags and walked out the door. As they were walking to school, Austin kept turning around to look at the man's house. They finally got to school right before the bell rang. Austin did his best to pay attention in his first few periods. Mr. Davidson's class had just ended, and it was time for lunch. The students all got up and left the room. Marcus looked back at Austin.

"I'll catch up with you," Austin said to Marcus. Marcus turned to go to lunch. Austin walked up to Mr. Davidson's desk.

"Can I ask you a question?" Austin asked.

"Of course. What can I do for you?" Mr. Davidson asked, putting papers away for his next class.

"What do you know of The Storm?" Mr. Davidson stopped what he was doing and turned to Austin.

"Well, I know he's not a very good God. The Gods were and are supposed to help us, protect us, and provide for us. I guess some Gods want us to worship them, and nothing more. Yin and Yang supposedly never got along. It's like they've been fighting since the beginning of time. It seems as if Yang convinced the other Gods that humans must worship and pray to them and nothing else. The Storm was the first God since Yin to come to Earth. He had made his mark. All the random hurricanes to show up were him. Hurricane Katrina, back in 2005, killed over 1,800 people. A hurricane back in 1900 hit Galveston, Texas, and killed 6000 to 12000 people, each one before, in between, and after. They are all him. He is a bad dude."

Austin was starting to get scared. "Do you think there's any way of stopping him?"

"A God?" Mr. Davidson laughed a little, "Not unless another God decides to step in. The Storm has left us alone for the most part. He sends random hurricanes over here to remind us he is in control. Whatever he's doing. It's working. People are scared, praying and worshiping out of fear, not faith." Mr. Davidson stood up and walked around his desk to Austin. "Why the sudden interest in the Gods? In The Storm?"

"Oh, no reason. I better get to lunch." Austin ran out of the classroom to go to lunch.

"What took you so long?" Marcus asked when Austin arrived.

"I was just asking Mr. Davidson some questions, that's all," Austin said as he sat down and pulled out his lunch. They all ate their lunch and finished the rest of the day—the final bell rang. Austin and Marcus packed up their schoolwork and walked out of their last period class toward the school entrance. They saw a large crowd by the front doors looking outside. They made their way to the front by slipping in between other students.

"Hey! That's my sister!" Austin yelled as he and Marcus ran outside to confront a group of guys that have Elsie trapped in a corner.

Austin and Marcus shoved their way to get in front of Elsie. Austin notices that these were the same guys that he and Marcus fought off when helping that older man earlier this week. Only now, there were a lot more of them.

"I knew we'd find you here. We saw you walk with this lovely little girl to this school a few days ago," the leader of the group said in a creepy, nasty voice. "I think it's about time you guys get what's coming to you."

"The only thing you guys are going to get is another ass whooping," Marcus said with fists in the air.

The leader of the group looked over to the three guys on his left and nodded forward. Marcus tried swinging, but he was no match for three grown men. One punched

Marcus in his stomach, and the other two grabbed him. They all started hitting him until he was on the ground. Teachers calling the police and gathered the students together to try to keep them safe.

"Your turn," the leader said, looking at Austin as he swung his fist and hit Austin across the face knocking him down.

Elsie started to scream in fear. The other members started to gang up on Austin, kicking him while he laid on the ground. Students started to record the whole interaction. These things don't usually happen around here.

Once Marcus was able to get up, he started to fight back, so one of the thugs left Austin and turned his attention to Marcus. This caught the attention of the thug kicking Austin which gave just enough time to reach into his pocket and pull out the coin the older man gave him. He carried it every day since that one day.

"I must be crazy," he said as he flipped the coin.

The thugs started kicking Austin again, but it didn't last long as, to Austin's surprise, a large raven flew down and flapped its wings in the thugs' faces and looked like it was attacking them. Austin couldn't watch long. He looked over to his sister where the leader thug was still standing.

"Now, what to do with you?" The leader asked.

Elsie quickly slapped him and yelled, "Leave me alone!"

This made the leader very angry, and he pulled his fist back.

"Why you little bitc…" before he could even finish, Austin jumped in the way.

"You touch her, and you're dead" Austin said.

A God Among Men

The thug grabbed Austin's shirt with his right hand. "You threaten me, boy?" the thug pulled his left hand back, but before he knew it, Austin used his left hand to swipe the thug's hand off of him. Austin slammed his right fist dead center of the man's chest. He flew back twenty feet in the air, hard and fast, and he smacked into the side of a car parked across the street. Everyone froze in shock. Police sirens were heard in the distance. The remaining thugs fled the scene. Austin just looked down at his hand. He could not believe what he just did.

He then looked back at Elsie. "Y-you, okay?"

Elsie just nodded her head slowly. She could not believe it either. No one believed what they just saw. Marcus got up slowly and just stared at Austin.

"Are you…"

Before Austin finished, "Yeah, I'm fine," Marcus said, staring at Austin.

Austin looked back at the rest of the students and teachers. Everyone was silent, just starring. Austin saw Mr. Davidson in the back, shocked and speechless, and in the front, Olivia. She took a few steps forward slowly. Austin looked down at the ground around him and back to Olivia. He could hear the police sirens getting closer. He turned and ran away.

"Austin!" Olivia yelled. But he did not stop or turn around.

He didn't run to work or home. He ran to the man's house where he was the night before. As he burst through the front door, it just looked abandoned.

"Here I am!" Austin yelled, "you said you'd be waiting here for me!" He fell to his knees and slammed his fist on the floor "where are you? I'm so confused. I don't know what just happened or who to talk to or where to go." He closed his eyes tight. "Please," he said.

"So, you're ready to know who you are?" said a voice. Austin opened his eyes and looked up as fast as he could. He was in a sea of clouds. And standing in front of him was the man from earlier.

"What was that back there? What did I do? I made a guy fly back like thirty feet in the air!" Austin yelled at the man.

"Don't you remember when I was getting attacked? The wind knocked that man down. You did that. You caused the wind to move." the man said.

"I did what now?" Austin asked. "Who are you?"

"That's the wrong question," the man said back to Austin.

Austin looked around for a little and took a second to think. He took a deep breath. "I'm going to regret this," he said softly, shaking his head. "Who am I?" he asked the man.

The man just smiled. "Right question. You are a God. You are more than a God. You are God and human. You were able to do that because you have power."

"What do you mean God and human," Austin asked.

"Your mother is Leah Kale, but your father is the God of Light and Life. You were created from his heart and soul. Born to Leah Kale."

Austin stood there confused, trying to comprehend what he was hearing. "My father? Brian Kale, is the God of Light? "

"Not him." the man cut Austin off. "Yes, Brian is your earthly father, and he did an amazing job raising you, but he is not your true father."

"Elsie and Ava. Are they like me, also? "

"They are Brian's children. Only you have God blood in you," the man said as he took a few steps toward Austin.

Austin was still trying to take it all in. "Well, how do you know all this?" Austin asked.

"I know a lot about the Gods' history," the man said.

"Okay, well, that doesn't explain anything," Austin replied, "and you think I can stop The Storm?"

"I know you can." he said as he put his hand on Austin's shoulder.

"How am I supposed to do that? Why can't you go stop him? You said you are a God," as Austin pointed at the man.

"It's not that simple. I am not strong enough right now."

"Right now?" Austin asked.

"That's a story for another time." the man said.

"Okay, but that still doesn't explain how I am going to fight a God," Austin said.

"Let's take a walk," the man said as he turned Austin to the side with his hand on his shoulder. Suddenly they weren't in the clouds anymore. They were in an abandoned little town that was destroyed by a hurricane not too far from Austin's hometown. Houses were destroyed, trees and other plants have overgrown the entire town. All you could hear was a train whistle not that far away.

"The Storm leveled this town. A few survived but abandoned this place. The rest didn't make it," the man said, walking next to Austin.

"That's so sad. This place is full of death and destruction."

"That's where you're wrong," the man said, grabbing Austin by the shoulders. "The Storm wants us all the think death and destruction lie in his path. Close your eyes."

"What?" Austin asked.

"Close your eyes." the man said again. Austin did as he was told.

"What do you hear?" the man asked.

"The train?" Austin asked. He opened his eyes.

"No, Austin, close your eyes and listen harder." the man said.

Austin closed his eyes again. He began to concentrate on his hearing. He began to hear the wind blowing and the leaves in the tree brushing against each other. He heard little animals running around. Small insects making noises and birds chirping.

"Now you are listening, Trees, plants, even the animals. This place is filled with even more life than before the storm hit. Yes, it's sad what happened to the humans here. But you can prevent this from happening anywhere else. Do you know what the most powerful thing in the universe is?" the man asked as he walked next to Austin.

"I don't know. The Gods?" he asked in reply.

"A story." the man said.

"A story?" Austin looked at the man like he was crazy.

"That's right. A story. More powerful than any of the Gods. You can't kill it. People love a story or hate the story because it scares them or because they don't want to believe it. Either way, everyone knows it. They live forever in books, songs, or word of mouth. They will still exist long after any human or God." The man stopped and looked at Austin. "Are you ready to start your story?" the man said as he began to walk toward the train tracks. Austin stopped walking and just looked at the man.

"This is where I leave you for now." The man kept walking.

"Wait, how am I supposed to do this on my own? I don't even know where to begin," Austin said.

"The light will guide you, Austin."

"What does that even mean?" Austin asked as the train got closer. The man walked over to the other side of the tracks.

"Who are you?" He yelled over the noise of the train whistle. The man turned back around.

"My name is Yin, and it was good talking to you, my son," Yin said right before the train passed in between them.

Austin didn't know what to do or say. Was he really talking with his birth father? The God of light? Austin was trying to look through the cracks of the train but couldn't see anything. He looked to his left and saw the end of the train coming. Just as the end of the train passed, Yin was gone. All he saw was a raven flying away.

Austin was speechless. He turned to run home a few towns over. He didn't even know what to think. Could it really be that his birth father was watching over him all these years from across the street? Does he even believe what the man was saying was true? What was he going to tell his mom and dad? So many questions ran through his mind.

Meanwhile, across the deep blue sea, in the eye of the endless hurricane, The Storm sat on top of a throne in a shrine dedicated to him. It was built by enslaved people he had been ruling over since he came to Earth.

One of his huntsmen ran up the golden stairs to his throne room. "Sir, you need to see this!"

A loud thunder crashed through the skies as The Storm looked angry at the huntsman. The Storm's two lions stood up and roared at the huntsman. "You bow before you address me!" The Storm roared.

"Yes, I'm sorry, my God." the huntsman bowed.

"What do you want." The Storm asked in his thunderous voice.

"You need to see this video. I believe he's the one Yang has been looking for." the huntsman pulled out a tablet and hit play.

He watched the video of Austin pushing the fully grown man back twenty feet in the air.

"Do we know who this is?" The Storm asked.

"It says some kid named Austin Kale. Looks like he lives in a small town just outside of Miami, Florida, in the United States."

"Find him and bring him to me," he said as he turned to walk back to his throne.

"Don't you think YOU should go get him?" said the huntsman.

The Storm froze in his steps. The loudest thunder crashed, and he turned around quickly and gave out a thunderous roar, and lighting flew from his hand and struck the huntsman, and he dropped dead where he stood. He turned to the other huntsmen. "Will this be a problem for anyone else?!" he roared. The other huntsmen just shook their heads no. "Good," The Storm sat on his throne. "Now it's time for a hunt."

The Storm closed his eyes and started spinning his hand around. The rest of the huntsmen ran down the hill side toward the ships. A large hurricane started to form over the ships. They got their four biggest ones and set sail for the United States.

Chapter 5

Homecoming

Austin ran all the way home. He busted into the front door. "Mom! Dad! I need to talk to you!" he yelled. To his surprise, his mom, dad, Elsie, Marcus, Olivia, Olivia's parents, and Mr. Davidson were all inside his house. They all stood up, and his mom, dad, and Elsie ran to hug him.

"Thank goodness you're okay," his mom said, not letting go of Austin. "You had me worried sick."

"Why? I was only gone a couple of hours," Austin said as he tried to get a breath with his mom hugging him so tight.

"Austin," She let him go. "It's been two days."

"Two days?!" He said with wide eyes and scratching his head. "No way."

Marcus and Olivia went to hug him. "We were all worried about you, man," Marcus said.

"Where were you!" Olivia yelled, punching him on his arm.

"Ouch!" Austin grabbed his arm to rub it. "It's kind of a long story."

"Come on, Olivia. I'm sure Austin needs some rest and alone time with his family." Olivia's mom said. Olivia and her parents walked toward the door. Her mom put her hand on Austin's shoulder. "I'm glad you are home safe."

"We're having a long talk tomorrow," Olivia said as she gave him a big hug. Austin began to blush. "I'm glad you are okay," Olivia said before she walked out the door.

Mr. Davidson walked up next. "If you ever need to talk, my door is always open."

Marcus walked out the door. He turned around. "I'm glad you're okay. I'll talk to you later." He closed the door behind him.

Austin turned back to his parents. "We need to talk."

"Elsie, go to your room," their dad said.

"No, she can stay. She should probably hear this also." Austin started to walk to the table. Once they all sat down Austin took a deep breath. "I don't even know where to begin. Well, first, I'm assuming you all have seen the video?"

"Yes, we watched it," his dad said.

"Quite a few times," his mom added. "How did you make him fly back that far?"

"How do I explain this?" Austin said. "Okay." he took a deep breath. "I am.." Austin laughed a little because he didn't believe he was about to say this. "I am part God."

Everyone looked at him, very confused.

"Are you drunk? Were you drinking?" his mom asked him.

"No, mom, I'm not drunk. I was able to make that guy fly backward because I think I have powers," Austin said, still trying to believe it himself.

Elsie grabbed a fork and put it on the table. "Can you make this fly?" she asked.

"I don't think that's how it works," Austin said. "I've never tried. Listen, I'm still trying to believe it myself."

"Where did you come up with this story?" Austin's mom asked.

"I was, umm, talking to my father," Austin said quickly.

"I'm sorry, did you just say your father?" Mrs. Kale turned to look at Mr. Kale.

"No, mom, it wasn't him," Austin said.

Now everyone was more confused.

"Listen, mom. I'm your son. But dad, I'm not your son. Well, I am, but I'm not. My father is the God of light. He said you are my earthly father and have raised me wonderfully. He told me that I was created from his heart and soul. I grew in mom's stomach and was born to both of you. But instead of dad's blood in me, I have God blood. Does that make sense?" Austin said.

Silence.

"Did you hit your head?"

"Are you crazy?"

"How am I supposed to respond to that?" Elsie and his mom wouldn't stop asking questions. Austin put his head down and closed his eyes and took a deep breath. He picked his head back up and continued to tell his parents and sister everything about the coin, the man he and Marcus helped, and everything that happened. Still loads of nonstop questions from Elsie and their mom. Only his dad was sitting there quietly, looking at Austin.

A God Among Men

"Dad? Why aren't you saying anything?" Austin asked.

He stood up and turned to the window and looked up at the house where the raven sat. "Honey, I need to tell you something."

"Are you okay?" Austin's mom responded.

"Before any of the kids were born, I went to see a doctor." He turned back to look at her. "I wasn't able to have kids."

"What do you mean you have three beautiful children," she said.

"Please, just let me finish. The night after I got the results, I went to the bar and drank, a lot. I couldn't have children. I was devastated. I got home from the bar, after you fell asleep. It felt like a dream, I remember getting out of the truck and dropping my keys. After I picked them up, I felt a hand on my shoulder and thought I saw a man with white eyes. Then everything went black. When I came to, I was in bed with you. I looked out the window and saw a raven fly away." Austin's dad said.

"Sweety, you just said you drank a lot. You were probably just drunk," she said as she stood up to give him a hug.

"But that's the thing. Once I woke up in bed, I felt great. I didn't feel drunk at all. I felt better than I have in a long time. I had a dream that night, and a bright light spoke to me and said Austin's name. A few weeks later, you picked it. It told me that my son would save the world. I went back to the doctor's the next day, and they didn't know how to explain it, but they said there was no sign of any problems in the first place." Mr. Kale said.

"So, you're saying our children are Gods?" she said in disbelief.

"No, just me," Austin interrupted. "Elsie and Ava, they are all you guys," pointing at his parents.

"You believe him?" Austin's mom asked her husband.

"I don't have any reason not to."
Austin gave him a little smile.

"You are still going to have to convince me that the God of light put a baby in my stomach, but for right now, I'll say that I believe you. What does that mean for you?" She asked, pointing at Austin.

"Well, this part you're not going to like. You know that God that came to Earth? The Storm?" Austin asked.

"That scary-looking man?" his mom asked back.

"Well, first, he's not a man. He's a God. An unbelievably bad and powerful God. And... I need to stop him."

"You have to stop a God? Why would I overreact to that?" Mrs. Kale said, still shocked by what she was hearing. "How are you supposed to stop him?"

"I'm not sure," Austin said, taking a deep breath.

"Where is he?" his dad asked.

"I think somewhere in Norway."

"Norway?! Across the sea?! You expect me to just let you, an almost eighteen-year-old, go to another country alone to fight a God?! That's where I draw the line." she said, crossing her arms in anger. "Son of a God or not, you are still my child, and you follow my rules."

"Mom, I need to do this. People are getting hurt and even dying all over the world." Austin said as he tried to comfort his mom. "I'm not leaving right now. I'm not even sure where to begin. I still need to graduate." Now Austin was just trying to tell his mom what she wanted to hear.

"I'm coming with you." his dad said.

"Dad, no, it could be dangerous."

"That's exactly why I'm coming. I need to keep you safe. Whenever you go, I'll be there." Austin's dad told him. Austin just nodded his head.

"Me too," added Elsie.

"No, Elsie, you need to stay here and keep mom and Ava safe. I can't trust anyone else to do that". Elsie was a little upset. But she just nodded and went and hugged her mom. Austin continued. "Everyone, stop being so down. I'm still here. I know things are weird right now but let's just finish out the school year and worry about everything else later".

"Let's all get some sleep. It's been a long day," Mr. Kale said.

The next morning everything seemed normal. Austin got up, showered, ate breakfast, and waited for someone, anyone, to bring up last night's conversation. There was still some disbelief in the air, but family trusts family, no matter what. That was something Austin's grandfather, Austin's dads' father, always said before he passed away. Mr. Kale started saying it a lot. Sometimes too much, but it's family. They have no reason to lie, and you have no reason not to believe them, even though the story can be the most ridiculous thing you've heard. Their mom walked out of the bedroom with Ava. She was drinking her bottle. Elsie was taking forever to get ready like always. Their dad was in the kitchen making breakfast for their mom and Elsie. He had already made breakfast for himself and Austin. Austin was happy. For once, he thought everything was normal again.

The door flung open "Good morning, Kale family!" Marcus yelled, walking into the house. "Breakfast smells great." Austin closed his eyes and just smiled, just as he was thinking... normal.

Marcus, Elsie, and Austin all left the house and walked to school. They passed the house that Yin was using. There was a for sale sign outside.

"It's about time they fix up and sell the house," Elsie said, and the three of them just kept walking, not turning back for anything. Austin wanted his life to get back to normal. Sometimes he didn't even believe what happened. Maybe it was all a big dream. They all got to school. It seemed less crowded than usual. Olivia ran up to Austin.

"We need to talk." she grabbed his hand and ran inside an empty classroom. Everyone was staring at him along the way.

"Why is everyone looking at me?" Austin asked, looking out the window of the classroom door.

"Probably because you Hulk punched a man into a car that was twenty feet away." Olivia responded.

"The school knows about that?" Austin asked looking back at Olivia.

"The whole world knows about it. It's all over the internet. How did you even do that?" Olivia asked.

"It's kind of hard to explain."

"I have time," Olivia replied. The first bell started to ring.

"Maybe another time," Austin said as he opened the door to go to class.

A God Among Men

Students in the hallway just stopped and looked at him. He started feeling a little nervous. As he was walking, one of the more popular girls in school came up to him. She always went for the big and tough football players. She always wore short skirts, but just long enough to follow school policy, and tight shirts with a pushup bra. You could tell when she was trying to flirt because she always tilted her head just a little and always twirled her hair, which was exactly what she was doing when she walked up to Austin. Olivia walked out and saw her talking to him. She shook her head, sighed, and marched away in the opposite direction.

"Hey Austin, you know that was so amazing what you did the other day," The girl said. "You must be so strong." as she twirled her hair.

"Uhm, thank you? How do you know who I am?" he said as he backed up into the lockers.

"I've always known who you were. I always had eyes for you." the girl kept stepping toward Austin. "Come say hi to my friends." The girl grabbed Austin around his arm and pulled him to her friends, the popular kids.

Marcus and Olivia were at the other end of the hall watching what was going on. Olivia was squeezing the ends of her notebook in anger. She did not like seeing him with another girl around his arm.

"Don't worry. He knows who his real friends are." Marcus said as the morning announcements were talking about the homecoming dance.

Austin could not go to any of his classes without his new lady friend holding onto his arm.

In Mr. Davidson's class, everything was going normal. Austin handed in his homework, took notes, and asked questions. It was a normal class for once. After class, the bell rang for lunch. The students all stood up and walked out the door. When Austin got to the lunchroom, he saw Marcus and Olivia sitting, waiting for him. Just as he took a step, "Hey you!" the popular girl yelled from her table. She stood up and ran to Austin and grabbed his arm again and brought him to her table to sit next to her.

"I guess we found out who his real friends are," Olivia said sadly as they ate their lunch quietly.

Elsie walked over. "Hey Marcus, hey Olivia."

"Hey, Elsie," they both said at the same time.

"Where's Austin?" Elsie asked as she sat down. Marcus just pointed over his shoulder. "With his new friends."

Elsie looked and saw the popular kids and Austin having lunch together with the popular girl literally all over him. The girl stood up and grabbed Austin's hand and pulled him out of the lunchroom. Lunch was about to end, and the students were all finishing up.

Olivia looked over and didn't see Austin. "Where did he go?" She asked Marcus.

"Maybe he went to class early?" Marcus said. It's not unusual for students to leave lunch early. they either hang out in the courtyard or sit and relax in the next classroom before everyone else gets there.

"Why?" Marcus asked Olivia.

"I want to ask him something," Olivia said as she grabbed her bag and left the lunchroom. She was looking all over for him.

She walked to his locker, to his next class, and checked in the courtyard. No sign of him anywhere. She was walking down the hallway toward her next class and heard a laugh coming from a classroom up ahead. She ran and opened the door. She stood there, shocked. She found Austin... kissing the popular girl in an empty classroom. Austin turned his head and saw Olivia. He pushed the popular girl off him.

"Olivia, wait! It's not what it looks like," Austin said. Olivia turned and ran down the hallway, upset, and started to cry. Austin ran out the door to see her running away.

"Sorry. I need to go," he said to the girl as he took off and ran after Olivia.

"Austin! Do not run from me! Don't you know who I am?" the girl screamed in a bratty little voice. She always got what she wanted and Austin running away was a slap in the face.

Olivia ran out the front door crying. Austin ran out shortly after her.

"Olivia!" he said, trying to catch up to her. "Please listen to me. It wasn't what it looked like."

"Oh really? Because it really looked like you both had your tongues down each other's throat!" she yelled through her tears. "I don't know what's been going on with you. You chose them over Marcus and me today. Even your sister asked where you were. I guess you're too cool for us now that you have some viral video?"

"No, it's not like that," Austin said, trying to get a few words in.

"Then what, Austin? I thought we were closer than that." It started to drizzle outside. "Me, you, and Marcus have been friends for how many years now? You just blew us off like we didn't matter."

"I sat with them because she pulled me over to them. And for once in my life, I felt like I had more friends than just you and Marcus. You both have other friends that you hang out with. I don't have anyone else. I wanted too actually be somebody today."

"You are somebody, to me. I was looking for you to ask if you wanted to go to homecoming with me, but now, I don't know." The rain started to pick up.

"Come on, let's get inside. It's starting to rain." Austin tried putting his arm around Olivia as they turned to walk inside, but she wouldn't let him. She was still angry about the kiss.

"I would love to go to homecoming with you," Austin said.

"Don't you need to ask your new girlfriend?" Olivia said with a little attitude.

"No way, she is not my girlfriend. I'm happy to say I'll never sit with them again. I do have one question though."

"What?" Olivia asked.

"If you liked me this whole time, why didn't you ever say anything to me? Sometimes it felt like you didn't know I even existed."

"I never knew what to say to you. You were always the coolest person to me. And I got nervous a lot when I was around you. Marcus made it easier because he always lightens the mood."

"Yeah, he's good with that," Austin said. "I really am sorry."

"It's okay," Olivia said as they gave each other a hug. "I'm still mad at you," she said as she punched Austin in the gut. Just as soon as they got to the door of the school, lightning struck the ground in front of them, knocking Austin and Olivia backward.

"Olivia!" Austin yelled.

"I'm okay!" she yelled back.

They got to their feet, ran to each other, and made sure they were okay. Austin was checking out his elbow, where he got a scratch from when he landed.

"Austin?" Olivia said.

"Yeah?" as he was still looking at his elbow.

"Austin, look," Olivia said, pointing at the roof of the school.

"What?" Austin picked his head up and saw four hooded men standing on the roof of the school.

"I don't suppose they're here to set up homecoming?" Austin said nervously.

One of them threw a bolas down at Austin, but he jumped out of the way. He grabbed Olivia's hand.

"RUN!" he screamed as they ran through the parking lot.

It was getting harder to see outside with the rain coming down. The fog was starting to set in, which made things worse. The hooded men jumped down and started chasing after them. Austin and Olivia hid between two cars.

"Do you think we lost them?" Olivia asked.

"I hope so," Austin said as he peeked around the car. He couldn't see anything because the rain was so heavy. Austin's and Olivia's phones started going off with a severe weather warning for a hurricane.

"I don't think this is a normal storm," Austin said, looking at his phone.

"Austin!" Yelled Olivia, as one of the men found them. Austin grabbed Olivia's hand again, and they ran back toward the school. The hooded man threw a bolas, and it wrapped around Olivia's ankles, causing her to trip and fall.

"Austin, help!" she yelled. Austin turned around and ran back to try and untie her ankles. The bolas was wrapped tight, but Austin was able to get it off.

"Austin, look out!" Olivia yelled as she pointed to all four men running toward them.

Austin stood up and yelled, "leave us alone!" He closed his eyes and pushed his hands forward, and a gust of wind from his hands blew all the men backward a few yards. The hooded men hit the ground hard. They all got up and ran away. Olivia was looking at Austin.

He turned around. "You okay?"

"Yeah, thanks," as she was still looking at him.

"Come on, before they come back." Austin helped Olivia up, and they ran back to the school. They were dripping wet. Everyone was staring at them when they walked inside.

"I need to tell you something." He said to Olivia. "Go find my sister and meet me at Mr. Davidson's room." Olivia nodded and went to find Elsie.

Austin went to find Marcus, and they all met up at Mr. Davidson's classroom. Austin, still dripping wet, walked in the room. Mr. Davidson was in the middle of teaching a class. He saw Austin soaked and looked out to see the other three kids standing there.

"Everyone, class is over early today. No homework," he said as he tried to rush everyone out of the room. Once everyone left, Olivia, Marcus, and Elsie walked in also. Austin turned to shut and lock the door. He then proceeded to tell everyone what he told Elsie and their Parents. Elsie was backing up everything he said.

"So that's why you were asking about The Storm the other day?" Mr. Davidson asked.

"Yeah," Austin replied.

"Because you have to fight him?" Mr. Davidson added. Austin just nodded.

"And that's how you pushed that thug guy back?" Austin nodded again.

"And again, just a few minutes ago!" Olivia added.

"Wait, what happened a few minutes ago?" Mr. Davidson asked while still trying to figure out why Austin and Olivia were all wet.

"There were four hooded men outside the school. They tried getting Austin and me. One of them threw something at my feet, and it wrapped around my ankles, and I fell. Austin came to help me, and as the men started getting close, he stood up and, well, pushed them all away without touching them." Olivia said as everyone was looking at Austin.

"Then they ran away," Austin added, "And we don't know if they will try again."

Mr. Davidson pulled out his phone and called someone.

"Right as it started raining, they showed up. I don't think that was just a coincidence. I think they were sent by The Storm." Austin said as he was walking around the classroom.

"You think he knows about you already?" Marcus asked.

"I'm not sure what to believe. But I asked Yin where to start, and all he said was the light would guide my way. Or something like that. Do any of you know what that means?" Austin asked.

"The Light would guide you? You mean like the sun?" Olivia asked.

"The sun lights half the world at a time. I'm not sure how that would guide you." Marcus said.

"Okay, something smaller, like a fire. Maybe a candle?" Austin said.

"There are a lot of candles in the world. How do we know which one?" Olivia asked.

"What about a flashlight? Or something like that. You said that the light would guide you, right? Well, a flashlight helps people see where they are going." Marcus said.

"Oh yeah, that's a good one. Okay, so if we stick to that, then we need to find a specific flashlight then?" Austin said.

Mr. Davidson hung up his phone and let the kids know they were canceling homecoming for right now. They do not want to risk the safety of any of the students. Austin then asked Mr. Davidson what his thoughts were on what Yin said.

"The light will guide you? I don't remember reading anything about a guiding lig... wait," he ran around his desk and pulled out a notebook from his work bag. "I remember seeing something in my great grandfather's journal when he was traveling the world." Mr. Davidson flipped through pages in the notebook. "Ah ha! Here it is," as he points to some of the notes on a page. "A lighthouse to guide lost souls to be with the Gods, The Lighthouse of Alexandria."

"Well, that sounds like a good fit to me. I do think we should explore other ideas, though." Austin said.

"That's great. What else do you know about that lighthouse?" Elsie asked.

"Not a lot. It was once the largest man-made structure in the world. Believed to light the way for loved ones who passed away to find their way to the Gods. But there are two very big issues with this."

"What's that? Olivia asked.

"The lighthouse was in Egypt." Mr. Davidson said.

"Egypt?! Great, how are we supposed to get there?" Marcus asked.

"Wait, what do you mean by it WAS in Egypt?" Elsie asked.

"That's the second issue. Long ago, it was damaged by three earthquakes and was submerged underwater. It hasn't lit the way for anyone in a very long time." Everyone was disappointed.

"Well, now what?" Marcus asked everyone.

"I'm not sure. Maybe Yin meant a different light house?" Austin said, shrugging his shoulders.

"Wait, is Yin the God of light?" Elsie asked.

"Yeah, why?" Austin said.

"What if he's the light that has to guide you?"

"I never thought of that, but why would he say that and not just say that he would guide me?" Austin asked.

"Well, how about we all do some research, see what we can find out, and meet up somewhere tomorrow and go over what we found out," Elsie suggested.

Everyone seemed to be on board with that plan. Time got away from everyone. Olivia missed her bus.

"You could always come to my house for a little while and get picked up from there if you want," Austin said.

"I would like that," she added as they both stood there blushing.

"Well, this is weird," Marcus said, standing between them.

Later that night, they all did their research. Elsie was in her room while Austin and Olivia were in the basement. Marcus was at his house, and Mr. Davidson was at his. Everyone was working hard, trying to find a light that fits the riddle. A perfect song for a school dance came on the radio while Austin and Olivia were researching. Austin stood up and held out his hand.

"Homecoming might have been canceled, but can I have this dance anyway?" Olivia couldn't help but smile. She grabbed Austin's hand and stood up, and they started dancing.

She laid her head on his chest. All she said was, "Best homecoming ever."

Chapter 6
The Hunt

Across the sea, The Storm sits on his throne. Huntsmen stand guard all around his throne room. One of his messengers runs up and bows,

"Sir, I got word from the first huntsmen who came in contact with the Austin Kale kid."

"And?" The Storm asked.

"The rumors are true. It appears he has superhuman-like abilities. Some even say God-like."

The Storm clenched his fist around the arm of his throne. "Did they get him?"

"Unfortunately, they did not, sir," the messenger said, lowering his head and backing up slowly.

"How is it that four trained men can't capture one little kid!?" The Stormed yelled as thunder crashed and lightning struck all around. He stood up and walked down from his throne. "Do I have to do everything myself?" just as soon as he got down the steps, he heard a raven's caw. He turned around and looked up and saw a raven flying in a circle. The raven flew straight down to the throne. When the raven landed on the throne, a cloud of white smoke appeared. As the smoke began to fade, Yin was sitting on The Storm's throne.

"I see you've been busy," Yin said, looking around the throne room and rubbing the arm of the throne.

"I see you've gotten old." The Storm said as he formed a lightning bolt in his hand and threw it at Yin. Yin's eyes began glowing white, and his hand began glowing as well. He quickly held his hand in front of him to block the lightning. When the lightning struck Yin's hand, it just burst into mist, slowly falling to the ground.

"You just strike first and talk later, don't you?" Yin asked The Storm. The Storm tried striking again. This time Yin caught it, spun around, and threw it back at The Storm's feet, causing an explosion. The Storm waved his hand in front of him to get rid of the smoke. Yin was standing right in front of him.

"So short-tempered, that will cause you to be your own destruction," Yin said.

"What do you want, Yin?" The Storm asked, annoyed.

"I came to give you a choice. Stop terrorizing the Earth, leave and never come back, or die."

"You can't kill me, Yin. You aren't strong enough. Even you know that." The Storm said with a deep chuckle.

"Oh, I wasn't talking about me. There is another." Yin said.

Storm's face turned serious.

"You think there is anyone that can match my power? Don't make me laugh," The Storm said.

"You already know who I'm talking about, Storm." Yin said.

"The boy? You think he's going to kill me?" Storm asked, feeling insulted.

"You killed yourself the moment you tried to rule these people, Storm," Yin said with such anger in his voice.

"I know, Yin. I know he's your son. I'm sure Yang would love to hear about him, maybe even pay him a visit," Storm said with an evil smirk on his face.

"Yang can't step foot on this Earth as long as I'm here. She will never get anywhere near Austin."

"Maybe I'll just have to change that." The Storm said.

"See you soon, Storm. Your days of ruling are over."

Yin transformed into a raven and flew away. The Storm was angrier than ever, "FIND THAT GOD MAN!" The Storm yelled.

The rest of his huntsmen, including two exceptionally large huntsmen captains, who The Storm had gifted with some of his powers, all got onto the remaining ships and set sail to hunt Austin.

Back home, everyone had a long night of trying to find a guiding light that fits what Yin told Austin. They all met back at Austin's house, but no one seemed to have any leads. They were digging through every history book, looking at every website, but no one could find anything.

"Wait! I might have found it! Everyone, look at this." Marcus said with excitement, "a red and white light house that sits on a stony island in Argentina. People call it the lighthouse at the end of the world. Doesn't that fit kind of what we're looking for?"

"Marcus, that is an awesome find, but I'm sorry, that's not it," Olivia said, looking at an old history book. Marcus looked disappointed. "The light house of Alexandria is the only lighthouse that was said to lead loved ones who passed away to be with the Gods in the afterlife."

"Yeah, but it was destroyed by three earthquakes," Elsie said.

"Yes, that's true, but look at these two pictures." Olivia pointed to the first, which was an old picture of the Lighthouse. There was a statue of a man holding a trident on top of the lighthouse.

"What's so special about that statue?" Marcus asked.

"Look at this." Olivia pointed to the second picture. It was of an old church. You could see inside the window. There was a statue of a man holding a trident. "What if the lighthouse did fall but didn't fully go underwater? What if the top part of the lighthouse, the part that actually lit the way for loved ones, never fell into the water at all?"

"That is a great theory, Olivia, but that's all it is, a theory. We can't just pack up and travel halfway across the world based on a theory." Mr. Davidson said. "Plus, if the actual lighthouse part is in a building, then I don't think it's lighting the way for anyone. An old lighthouse like that needs sunlight to work or a fire burning at the top of the lighthouse."

Disappointed looks filled the room as everyone sat back in their seats.

"Even after all this research, we are still lost. Yin hasn't been seen since the day he left. I can't ask him for help. I don't know what I'm supposed to do!" Austin said angrily, slamming his fist down on the table.

A God Among Men

Olivia got up and walked over to Austin and rubbed his back. "Hey, we will figure this out."

"I know, it's just frustrating," Austin said, as he ran his fingers through his hair.

"Let's all just take a break and meet back here in a day or two. We will pick up where we left off then. Okay?" Mr. Kale said. Everyone agreed and left the house.

"Call me if you need me or anything, okay?" Olivia said to Austin right before she left.

"Come on, even a God needs rest," Austin's dad said as he helped Austin up out of his seat.

Everyone went to bed while Austin stayed awake in his room. He was lying there, replaying everything that everyone said that night. He was doing research on his laptop. His eyes widened, and he sat right up. He ran out of his room. "Dad, wake up!" He yelled as he ran to the kitchen table. He was flipping through book after book, trying to find a picture. "DAD!" he yelled again.

His parent's door opened. "I'm up, I'm up," his dad said, yawning and rubbing his eye. "You do know it's two in the morning, right?" his dad said.

"No, I didn't realize that, sorry. I think I found a clue that leads to the lighthouse. Look at this," Austin showed his dad a picture of a wall with hieroglyphics on it.

"This is telling the story of the lost souls finding their way to the Gods. And look," Austin pointed to the top of the lighthouse. "A man with a trident."

"Okay, but that doesn't explain how the lighthouse can light the way inside of a church." his dad said, taking a closer look at the pictures.

"That had me stumped also. So, I started looking up pictures of the church. There is a glass window on the roof of the church, directly over the statue. The sun has to be in a specific spot for the sun light to shine through the roof and hit the lighthouse," Austin said.

"Okay, that's a good find, but like your teacher said, it's just a theory," his dad said, laying his hand on Austin's shoulder.

"All we are going to have are theories dad. It's not like we're going to find something that says, 'Hey, come here. This is what you're looking for.' This is the best we have," Austin said.

"Okay, I'm not going to argue with a God," his dad said with a little laugh. "So, when does the sunlight shine through the roof?"

"So, Yin said the light will guide me, right?" Austin said.

"Yeah," Austin's dad said back to him.

"Well, now look at this. There is writing on the wall of the church." Austin pointed at a picture.

When I'm at my highest, I will be your guide.

"Okay? So, what does that mean?" his dad asked.

"My guess is it's talking about the sun. When the sun is at its highest point, it will be the guide. The sunlight and the light house. It just makes sense. The sun is at the highest point in the sky on the longest day of the year," Austin said.

"So, when is that?" His dad asked.

"Well, the longest day of the year in Egypt is the summer solstice. June 21st. If I had to guess, whoever built the church around the lighthouse designed it to still light the way on the longest day of the year when the sun is at the perfect position in the sky," Austin said to his dad.

His dad didn't say anything for a little bit. He kept looking at the pictures and mumbling to himself Austin's theory. "You know. That actually makes sense," his dad said back to him. Austin smiled. "But it's a very big leap. If we fly all the way to Egypt to go to this church and we're wrong, then we just wasted all that time."

"Okay, but if we don't go and it's right, then we are screwed and would have to wait a one more year," Austin said.

He made a very excellent point. His dad stood there scratching his head. "Okay." He said.

"Okay? So, we're going to go?" Austin asked.

"Yes, but you still need to finish out the school year," his dad said as he walked back to his bedroom.

"Yes, of course!" Austin said with excitement. Austin yawned and stretched. He walked back to his room and laid in bed and fell right to sleep.

The next day was a school day. Austin woke up like usual and showered and ate his breakfast. He and Elsie always waited for Marcus in the morning, but this morning Marcus didn't show up at the house. It was getting late, so Austin and Elsie left to go to school. It was foggy outside.

"Is this normal weather?" Elsie asked Austin as she moved closer to him.

"Yeah, it always gets a little foggy this time of year," Austin said, just looking around. "Marcus probably went right to school."

Austin and Elsie arrived at school. Elsie walked to her locker and to where her friends were. Austin walked to his classroom. Class started, but Marcus was not there.

Austin just thought he stayed home sick and didn't think anything else if it. He continued through the school day. It was time for Mr. Davidson's class. Austin walked into the room, ready to tell Mr. Davidson what he had discovered last night. To Austin's surprise, there was a substitute teacher.

"First Marcus and now Mr. Davidson? With recent events, I don't think this is just a coincidence," he said to himself.

He got through the class, and now it was time for lunch. Maybe he could talk to Elsie and Olivia and figure out what's going on. He got to the lunch table and sat down and opened his bag and started eating his lunch. He was watching the lunchroom doors waiting for Elsie or Olivia to walk in, but neither of them did. Now Austin was starting to get worried. He got up and went out of the lunchroom. He walked down where Elsie's friends were.

"Have any of you seen Elsie?" Austin asked.

"Yeah, she was here earlier, and last period she went to the bathroom but never came back. Is everything okay?" One of Elsie's friends asked.

"I'm not sure," Austin said as he ran down the hallway. He ran to Olivia's first-period teacher, "Was Olivia here today?" Austin asked.

"I'm afraid I haven't seen her at all today. She must be sick." the teacher said.

"Yeah... sick," Austin said with concern as he walked out of the room confused. First, Marcus doesn't walk into their house in the morning, then a substitute teacher for Mr. Davidson, Olivia also didn't show up to school, and now Elsie was missing. Austin tells himself that he cannot call his mom or dad and worry them, but what if they are in danger?

Austin ran out the front door and ran straight home. The fog was even thicker, and it started to drizzle. He ran through the front door of his house.

"Austin! Are you out of your mind? You scared the crap out of me. Why aren't you in school?" his mom asked.

"Where's dad?"

"Relax, he just got out of the shower. Is everything okay?" His mom asked as she stood up to check on Ava, who was eating cheerios.

Austin's dad walked out of his bedroom after just getting dressed. "Austin? Why aren't you in school?"

Austin proceeded to tell his parents about Marcus, Olivia, Mr. Davidson, and Elsie going missing.

"We need to call the police!" his mom said.

"And tell them what? That our son has friends who did not show up to school and had a substitute teacher?" Mr. Kale asked. "Come on, let's go check Marcus' house." Austin's dad grabbed his keys, and they went to the truck to drive to Marcus' house.

It was so hard to see anything with the fog that they almost crashed a few times. When they got there, they saw the door cracked open. They ran inside and found Marcus' house was a complete mess. The furniture was flipped over and things were thrown all over the place.

Austin yells, "I have to check on Olivia and her family!"

"You go. I'll stay here and see if I can find anything that can help," Austin's dad said to him as he threw him the keys. Austin ran to the truck. Almost fumbling the keys, he got in and drove toward Olivia's house. He was panicking so much that his hands were shaking. Once he got to her house, he ran and kept knocking on the door until Olivia's mom answered.

"Austin? What a surprise. Everything okay?" she asked after seeing how shook-up Austin was.

"Did Olivia leave for school this morning?"

"Yes, she did. Did you not see her at school?" her mom asked. "Austin?" She asked again, but Austin just turned around and started walking toward the street.

He got in the car and drove back toward Marcus' house. He was so in shock at what was happening. He would never have thought that his family and friends would be in danger, even after he found out who he really was. He stopped at a stop sign and waited for a little while, just thinking, hoping everyone was okay. He realized he needed to do everything he could to help his friends. He started to drive forward, but a truck came speeding through the stop sign and T-boned the truck he was in. Another truck came and T-boned the other side. Austin was stuck. His ears were ringing, and everything was spinning. He hit his head hard with the first hit. He was looking side to side, trying to figure out how to get out of this. The two trucks backed up. Austin looked forward and saw another larger truck coming head-on. They hit the truck Austin was in so hard the truck flipped over. Austin was bleeding and bruised everywhere. He looked out the broken truck door window and saw a large man walking toward the truck.

Austin, through the pain, quickly unbuckled his seat belt and fell to the roof of the upside-down truck. The large man ripped the truck door off with ease. The man bent over and looked inside and saw Austin crawling out the other side of the truck. The large man, with one hand, picked up the front of the truck and flipped it over. Now there was nothing between Austin and him. Austin tried to get up and run for cover. Holding his side and limping he ended up falling. As he hit the ground, the gold coin with the raven fell out of his pocket. He tried crawling for it, but the large man grabbed his legs and pulled him away from the coin. Austin rolled over and tried kicking the man away, but it wasn't working. The man picked Austin up by his head. Austin was screaming in pain. With Austin's good arm and all his strength, he hit the man in the face. The man dropped Austin and staggered a bit. Austin grabbed a piece of glass on the ground and held it close. The large man reached down to pick Austin up again. This time Austin rolled over and slammed the glass shard into the large man's chest. Austin was dropped and fell to the ground. That was just enough time for Austin to crawl to the coin and flip it.

The large man grabbed the piece of glass and pulled it out of his chest. He started to walk toward Austin again. The man got closer and made a lightning bolt appear in his hand and was about to throw it at Austin. Austin rolled to his side and covered his face... but nothing happened. Austin turned over and saw Yin kneeling next to him with smoke behind him. He took the blow for Austin.

"You okay?" Yin asked. Austin nodded his head. Yin stood up and looked at the large man. "Big mistake attacking my son and his friends." Yin's eyes started to glow white. He made a fist and slowly opened his hand. Austin saw a ball of light through his fingers. He shot his hand forward, and a white beam of light came out of his palm, and the large man went flying back. He slammed into a tree. And fell to the ground. Yin helped Austin up to his feet.

"What the hell was that?" Austin asked, pointing at the tree.

"Another time," Yin said as he turned around quickly. He saw more of the hooded men running toward them. They were surrounded.

"There's a lot more of them than us," Austin said.

"Yes, but they aren't Gods," Yin said as he turned back to Austin. He laid his hand on Austin's forehead, and he closed his eyes. Suddenly Austin was healed. No more bleeding or bruises. His side and his leg felt great. Some of the hooded men got close. Austin and Yin were fought back. Austin was throwing punches, fighting the huntsmen as they ran toward him. Eventually, Austin was able to have the wind blow any way he punched. He didn't know how he was doing it, but he didn't question it at that moment. Yin was shooting beams of light out from his hands. Each huntsman that was hit turned into a cloud of black smoke, and the smoke sank into the Earth.

"There's too many of them!" Austin yelled. "I can't keep this up."

"When I tell you to, jump." Yin jumped into the air and right before he slammed his palm onto the ground, he yelled jump, and Austin did just that. A wave of white light traveled outwards in a large circle hitting all the huntsmen and turning them to smoke. Austin looked around and saw there weren't any more men around them.

"Let's start with that from now on, okay?" Austin said, catching his breath. "Where have you been this whole time?"

"I was visiting an old friend," Yin said as he walked to the middle of the intersection. He held his hands up and started mumbling something with his eyes closed. Austin looked around and saw everything around them was being restored. Broken cars, streetlights, houses. Everything was back to normal, and anyone that saw anything suddenly forgot what had happened. "This weather is terrible," Yin said as he waved his hand, and the fog cleared up, the rain stopped, and the sun was shining.

"Just like that? One wave of your hand, and you think you can fix everything? My friends are still missing. If you had stayed, none of this would have happened." Austin said in anger.

"Relax, I'm going to help you get your friends back," Yin said.

"I don't even know where to begin," Austin said.

Yin just turned to point at a van. "Two of them are in there."

Austin ran over to a van the huntsmen were driving. He opened the back door and saw Marcus and Olivia lying down. Yin walked over and touched both of them, and they woke up instantly.

"Austin?" Olivia asked, as she started to tear up. Austin jumped in and hugged both Olivia and Marcus.

"I was so worried about you guys." he said.

"Uhh, Austin, that guy we saved at the beginning of the school year is behind you," Marcus said, pointing at him.

"Right, well, I guess it's about time." Austin climbed out of the back of the van. He helped Olivia out. Marcus climbed out himself.

"Olivia, Marcus, meet Yin. Yin, Olivia, and Marcus."

"It's a pleasure to meet both of you," Yin said, shaking both of their hands. "Especially the one who took my son's heart," he said to Olivia as he winked.

Marcus and Olivia couldn't believe they were looking at the all-powerful God of Light, Yin.

"Okay, enough," Austin said, "we still need to find Mr. Davidson and Elsie."

"You guys get back to his house," Yin said, pointing at Marcus, Olivia, and Austin. "I will meet you there."

Austin, Olivia, and Marcus all got into the truck, and drove back to Marcus's house. Austin told Marcus what happened today the whole way there. Once home, Marcus jumped out of the car and ran inside to find Austin's dad began cleaning up.

"Thank you," Marcus said as he hugged Mr. Kale. "I'm glad my parents weren't home."

"Of course. I'm just glad you guys are okay," Mr. Kale said. Olivia and Austin walked in, and Mr. Kale ran up to hug his son.

"Where's Elsie?" he asked Austin.

"We don't know where she or Mr. Davidson are." Austin said.

"Okay, well, let's go out and look for them."

"We can't yet," Austin said to his dad. "Yin said he was going to meet us here."

"Yin? Like the God?" his dad asked.

They heard a knock on the door, and Austin opened it. "Mr. Davidson!" he yelled and gave him a hug. "Are you okay? Where were you? How did you get here?" Austin was asking so many questions.

"He saved me," pointing behind him as Yin walked into the house.

"Who is that?" Austin's dad asked Austin.

Austin brought His dad over to Yin, "Dad, meet my dad, and dad, meet my dad," Austin said, introducing his dad to Yin.

"My brain hurts trying to understand that," Marcus whispered to Olivia.

Mr. Kale shook Yin's hand. "Thank you for everything."

"No. Thank you. You are the one who raised him. You will always be his dad," Yin said back to him.

Mr. Davidson sat down and told everyone how men showed up at his house, attacked him, and kept him there. "They were waiting for a van to come to get us. After a few hours, I saw a bright light outside, and the front door flung open, and this guy walked in," pointing to Yin. "It was amazing. He just raised his hand, and everyone inside just dropped to the floor. The next thing I knew, he touched me, and I felt great. No more pain. He told me who he was and that we needed to leave. I wasn't going to ask any questions, and now we are here."

"I am so glad you are safe, Mr. Davidson. But we still need to find Elsie," Austin said. "I can't have anyone else get hurt. Only Yin and I will go," Austin said.

"We will cover more ground if we all go. We all want to help," Austin's dad said.

Austin just agreed. They all sat down and tried to figure out where to start looking for Elsie. Mr. Kale started making dinner for everyone while they were getting a plan together. After everyone ate, Marcus and Olivia helped clean up. Yin was leaning on the wall next to the front door.

"We don't have this where I'm from," he said to Austin.

"Don't have what?" Austin asked.

"Family gatherings. Talks. Laughs." he said, looking around at everyone.

"You do here. You are always welcome here anytime. I mean, you are my dad. You're family".

Yin turned his head to the door.

"What is it?" Austin asked.

"Shh," Yin said to everyone holding his hand out to have everyone stop what they were doing. He turned back to the group. "Everyone out the back door, now!"

They all got up and rushed to the back door. Marcus opened the door, but there was a huntsman standing there waiting. Marcus ducked, and Austin pushed his hand forward, and a gust of wind pushed the huntsman back and made him flip over the back fence.

"Man, that never gets old," Marcus said as Austin pushed him out the back door. Everyone ran through the back gate to the woods behind the house.

"Where's Yin?" Austin asked.

"He never came out," Olivia said.

Yin was still inside. He opened the front door. There were at least fifty huntsmen out front, including another very large one. He was holding Elsie, who was tied up, over his shoulder.

"We just want the boy. Then you can have her." Elsie was scared, crying, and trying to scream through the tape over her mouth.

"You all made a big mistake coming here tonight." Yin was walking down the front porch steps with his hands out wide. "Let the girl go, and I will think about letting you all walk away from this."

A God Among Men

Austin ran back through the house and out the front door. "Elsie!" He yelled as he saw her.

"Get him!" the large man ordered as the rest of the huntsmen ran toward the house.

Yin closed his eyes, and when they opened, they were glowing white. He walked to the edge of the street. Both hands began glowing white. He slammed his hands down on the ground. Light energy traveled through the ground from his hands. The light energy shot out of the ground and struck multiple huntsmen. Yin stood back up. He held his hand out and a staff of light energy formed in his hand. He grabbed the staff with both hands and began fighting off huntsmen as they got close. With each hit, it blasted a huntsman back like a small explosion hit their chests. Yin spun the staff in his hand fast and threw it. The staff began flying in a big circle around him. Hitting huntsman as it spun around. For the few that made it through, Yin just shot them with a beam of light from his hands and eyes. Austin was watching, not realizing that some of the huntsmen were climbing over the side of the porch railing. Olivia could see this from the woods.

"Austin!" she yelled, and Austin turned to see them climbing up. He ran over and kicked the first one off the side of the porch and punched another. He jumped down and tried running to the man holding Elsie. He got tackled in the process. There were quite a few men holding him down. He couldn't punch or kick his way out.
Yin held his hand out behind him. The staff stopped spinning and flew back into his hand. There was a group of huntsmen running toward Yin. Once the staff was back in his hand, he slammed the staff on the ground in front of him. A wave of light traveled from the staff, crashing into

the group of huntsmen in front of him. Yin turned and saw Austin on the ground. He threw the staff, and it hit the huntsmen holding him down. Austin got up and looked around and saw that any remaining huntsmen ran or drove away, including the large one with Elsie.

"Elsie!" Austin screamed as he fell to his knees in the middle of the street with tears rolling down his face. "She was right there. And I couldn't get to her."

Mr. Kale and the rest of the group ran out of the woods. Austin's dad knelt next to him. "We will get her back. Because her big brother won't stop until she's safe," Mr. Kale said, holding back fear for Austin's sake.

Olivia knelt next to Austin as well. "She will be okay. She's a tough girl. We will find her." She hugged Austin tight.

Chapter 7
The Big Game

"How could you?" Austin said, making fists on the cold street ground. The streetlights started to flicker. "How could you let them take her?!" he yelled as he stood up and walked over to Yin. "You, this all-powerful God. Why didn't you go right for the man holding my little sister?!"

The weather started to change fast. The wind started picking up. The clouds started spinning. The swings at the park started to swing back and forth by themselves. All the streetlights and the neighbors' outdoor lights were flickering. Some of them burst and broke.

"YOU let them get away! YOU were nowhere around when they came and took everyone! YOU aren't helping me with any of this. You come down here, drop a bomb on us and tell me I'm some sort of God, and then you vanish? I didn't know what to do or where to start!" Austin yelled with such anger as he kept poking Yin's chest. Yin just stood there, letting Austin get it all out. Olivia walked up and grabbed Austin's hand. Austin turned quickly, so much anger on his face. Austin saw he was scaring Olivia. He looked up at his dad and then at Marcus and Mr. Davidson. He only saw fear on everyone's face. Austin started to cry more as he fell back down to his knees. "I should have saved her." he said as he cried.

Yin knelt and put his hand on Austin's shoulder. "We will get her back. You have my word." Yin stood back up. "Let's all get cleaned up. We have a lot of work to do."

Marcus and Mr. Davidson went back to their homes to get cleaned up and rest a little before meeting back at Austin's house. Olivia went back with Austin and his dad. They walked into the house as Austin's mom walked out of the baby's room after putting her down for the night. Mrs. Kale saw Austin, Olivia, and Mr. Kale, but not Elsie.

"Where…"

Before she could finish, Mr. Kale hugged her, "We will find her," he said. Austin's mom started to cry. Everyone was worried about Elsie. Their dad and Olivia were talking in the living room. Yin was sitting outside on the front porch, looking up into the sky.

Austin was in his baby sisters' room, just watching her sleep. "Don't worry, Ava. I will bring our sister home." he whispered and kissed Ava on the forehead. He walked out of the room and went out to the porch to sit next to Yin.

"I need to show you something," Yin said as Austin sat down. Yin waved his hand in front of him, and everything around them other than the bench they were sitting on began to crack and crumble. Giant pillars shot up from the ground around them. Beautiful mountains and trees appeared in the distance. Strange creatures were flying in the sky and roaming the ground. They were in an outdoor temple, in a paradise.

"Where are we?" Austin asked.

"This is one of the first planets we created. Peaceful. Beautiful. Free." Yin said.

"What happened to it?" Austin asked.

Yin just bowed his head. "Yang happened."

"Your sister?" Austin asked.

"That's right," Yin said.

Austin looked up as the sky started to turn black. Like a wave of darkness was covering the planet they were on. A pillar of black smoke was falling from the sky. Once it hit the ground, any creature around it dropped dead instantly. Out of the black smoke walked the most beautiful woman. Long black hair. Black robe with a hood. Eyes so black they looked empty. Tattoos covered her body, and Austin took notice of a black owl on her right arm.

"Is that...?"

"Yang," Yin said before Austin could finish. "The Goddess of darkness." Yin looked Austin in the eyes. "The Goddess of death."

"Why are you showing me this?" Austin asked. He looked back and saw Yang destroying the planet. Trees were burning. Mountains were falling. Creatures were dying.

"I'm showing you this because this is what will happen to your world if Yang comes."

"Okay, so how do we stop that from happening?" Austin asked.

"I made it so Yang can never come to the Earth. I'm the only thing stopping her. She has been trying for one thousand lifetimes. You've seen what The Storm can do. How powerful he is. To her? He's nothing, just a messenger. He's rolling out the red carpet for Yang and the other Gods and Goddesses. His brothers and sisters. The Storm is trying to make it so Yang can come to Earth. Which means he needs to get rid of me... and you." Yin told Austin.

"Okay, but why can't you stop him? Why can't you stop any of them?" Austin asked.

"I'm not strong enough to fight any God right now," Yin said.

"What do you mean right now?" Austin asked.

"The reason I'm not strong enough right now is because I'm using most of my power to keep Yang away. As long as Yang can't get to you, you and your world are safe. The moment I let up, she will come and kill this planet."

"Okay, so how do you want me to kill a God?" Austin asked.

Yin spun his hand in a big circle, and a portal appeared in front of them. "Come with me," Yin said as he walked through. Austin looked back at Yang. Yang quickly turned her head and looked Austin straight in his eyes. Austin turned pale. Like his soul left his body. She shot dark energy from her hands at Austin. He jumped through the portal, and it closed.

Austin fell to the ground screaming, grabbing his leg. Yin turned around and saw Austin on the ground. "What happened?!" Yin asked.

"Yang saw me! She shot some sort of black smoke at me, and it must have hit me as I jumped through the portal."

"She saw you? But that wasn't real. That was in the past." Yin said as he hovered his hand over Austin's leg, healing it. There was a terrible-looking burn on his leg.

"Well, it felt real to me!" Austin said.

"She must be more powerful than I thought if she can see you in a vision. We need to be more careful." Yin said as he finished healing Austin's leg. Yin helped Austin up. Austin looked around. They were now in what looked like an ancient city inside a mountain.

"Quickly, this way," Yin said as they walked into a cave. "I'm sure you have heard of this," Yin said, pointing to a sword made of a raven's wing.

"Aggon's sword!" Austin said as his eyes widened.

"Yes. Also known as the only thing that can kill a God. I created it before Yang tried coming to Earth. Yang and the other Gods believe this sword has been destroyed. You need to find it," Yin said.

"Can't you just tell me where it is?" Austin asked.

"I'm afraid I can't. I seem to have lost some of my memory. The last person to have it was Aggon." Yin said.

"But he died centuries ago. He can't exactly tell me where to go." Austin replied.

"Think Austin, you are a smart kid. You will find it." Yin said, putting his hand on Austin's shoulder.

Austin was thinking hard. His eyes widened, and he looked at Yin. "The lighthouse! What if all this time he's been leaving clues?"

"Sounds like a good place to start," Yin said as he walked over to Austin. He put his hand on the side of Austin's head and his thumb on his forehead. Austin closed his eyes, and when he opened them, they were back on the porch.

Olivia came out front. "We were looking all over for you," she said.

Austin looked at Yin, "We, uh, went for a walk."

"Mr. Davidson and Marcus are here, come on," Olivia said as she waved her hand toward the house.

Austin began to walk inside and turned back to Yin. "Are you coming?"

"No, you go. This is your family. I'll stay out here," Yin said as he looked back to the sky.

Austin just looked for a little and then went and grabbed Yin's arm. "You are my family also. Don't worry. We will get your memory back."

Once everyone was inside, Austin's dad cleaned off the table, and everyone sat down. "Okay, so how do we get Elsie back? Where is she? How does Austin defeat The Storm? I believe those are the top three questions that need to be answered. No secrets from anyone. Any ideas are welcomed."

Austin looked at Yin. Yin just nodded. Austin stood up and went to his book bag. "I have an answer for the last question. But it's going to bring up a lot more questions." Austin said, pulling a book out of his bag. He flipped it open to a certain page and laid it in the middle of the table.

Mr. Davidson sat up and looked at the page "Aggon's Sword?"

"That's right, The sword of Aggon. Also known as a God-killing weapon." Austin said as he looked back at Yin.

"I'm sorry, Austin, but no one has seen it since Aggon. That was centuries ago. Who knows if it still even exists?" Mr. Davidson said.

"It exists," Yin said as he walked up to the table. He had everyone's attention. "The sword is a part of me. I would know if it was destroyed."

Austin's mom turned to Austin. "You said it would bring up other questions. What are they?"

"Where is it? How do we find it? And how do I get close enough to The Storm for me to use it without him killing me first?" Austin said.

The whole room went silent. The thought of Austin fighting and dying didn't sit well with everyone.

"Well, what about the lighthouse? That has to be a clue for something, right? What if it leads to the sword?" Mr. Kale asked.

"That's what I was thinking, but just know that if we are wrong, we wasted all that time. I think we still need to try and figure out where else it could be. Like a backup plan." Austin said.

"Excellent idea," Mr. Davidson said. "I'll dig through some old books I have at home and in the library."

"What about Elsie? Yin, would you have any idea where she would be?" Austin asked.

"It's not good. If I know The Storm, he will want her close. Somewhere he could keep an eye on her himself. He wouldn't want his men messing anything up. He has a reason to make Austin go look for him."

"It's working," Austin said.

"Don't play by his rules. He won't kill her. Her being alive is the only thing he has to force you to go after him. It's all part of his plan. Find the sword. Then we will have the upper hand to go get him."

"As much as I hate that plan, I have to agree with Yin." Austin's dad said, "I want Elsie back just as much as anyone, but we can't risk losing anyone else. If the sword is the best chance we have, I won't stop looking for it."

"No time to waste then," Mr. Davidson said as he stood up and grabbed his things to go home.

"Wait," Austin said, stopping Mr. Davidson. "We all need to be extra safe now. I can't have anyone else get hurt because of me."

Everyone agreed as they all started to get ready to leave.

"I do hope everyone will be able to make it to my football game tomorrow. It's a big game. It could help me with getting into college." Marcus said.

"Of course, we will be there," Olivia said.

"We wouldn't miss it for the world," Austin said, "You are going to do great."

Everyone left the house. Austin's dad was still sitting at the table. "Everything okay, dad?"

"I just can't believe this happened to my little girl." Austin's dad said, putting his hands in front of his face.

"It's a good thing she has the best family in the world looking for her. We will find her. You heard Yin. We will get her back alive. I won't let anything happen to her." Austin said as he put his hand on his dad's back. His dad rubbed tears away from his eyes. He stood up and hugged Austin. His mom walked over and joined the hug.

"Everything will be okay." Mr. Kale said. "Let's get some sleep. Marcus needs our support tomorrow."

Everyone was back at their houses, trying to fall asleep. The only thing on their minds was Elsie, The Storm, and the sword.

The next morning Austin woke up and got ready for school. Marcus walked in and just froze, "Usually, Elsie is sitting here to greet me. I can't wait to get her back."

"We will," Austin said. "Come on, let's get to school."

Austin and Marcus walked to school in silence. Elsie would usually do all the talking. As Austin walked through the hallway, other students kept saying, "Sorry to hear about Elizabeth" and "I hope she's okay." It appears every single student was talking about it.

Marcus could see it was bothering Austin. "Dude, you just have to breathe." Austin pushed Marcus to the side of the hallway to talk in private.

"How do they know? We didn't tell anyone what happened. How is it that every student knows she's missing?" Austin's said.

Mr. Davidson was walking fast through the hallway. He saw Austin and Marcus standing next to the lockers. He went over to them and took them to his classroom. Olivia was talking to one of her friends and saw that.

"I got to go," she said and ran off after them. Mr. Davidson got them in the room and closed the door. Olivia, right behind them, opened the door and got inside. "What is going on?" Olivia asked. "Why are the three of you pushing through everyone in the hall?"

Mr. Davidson pulled out a newspaper and laid it on the desk they were standing around.

LOCAL TEEN KIDNAPED

That was the headline with a picture of Elsie on the front page. "How does the news know about this?" Austin said, getting angry. "We didn't talk to anyone."

"That's not all." Mr. Davidson pulled out his phone and pulled up the news on an app on his phone. There was a news story talking about a large man carrying a young girl that was tied up with tape over her mouth. Someone in a neighboring home was able to record her being put into the back of a van from their house. "Everyone knows now." Mr. Davidson said. Everyone just looked at Austin.

"Now what?" Marcus asked.

"Nothing, there's nothing we can do about it," Austin said. "We just need to take it one day at a time."

The bell rang for first period to start. Austin got to his class, and when he walked in, everyone was silent. He sat at his desk, and a few of the students went up to him to say sorry for what had happened to Elsie. Austin just nodded and said thank you. Next period, a few more students also said sorry. Now it was starting to bother Austin.

Mr. Davidson's class was next. Austin was one of the first students in the room since his class right before was across the hall. He sat down at his desk. Marcus walked in and sat at his desk on the other side of the room. One by one, students walked into the room, and one by one, as they passed Austin, they said sorry. Mr. Davidson and Marcus were keeping a close eye on him. Austin felt like it was never-ending. As each student said sorry, Austin's fists got tighter and tighter. The next student walked into the room and went to say sorry to Austin.

"Shut up!" Austin yelled as he slammed his fists down on his desk. When he slammed his fists down, every desk in the classroom was pushed away from him. The lights started to flicker and break in the whole school. Olivia saw this in her classroom and knew something was wrong.

"Would everyone just shut up already? Leave me alone!" Austin yelled.

"Okay, everyone out, nothing to see here. No talking about what just happened." Mr. Davidson said as he jumped up out of his seat to get all the students out of the room. Marcus ran over to Austin to try and calm him down. Mr. Davidson directed all the students to another classroom for this period with a different teacher. He ran back down the hallway to his room and closed the door behind him.

"Austin, you have to control yourself." he said as he pulled his chair up to Austin's desk.

"I just can't take everyone saying something about Elsie like she's dead," Austin said as he grabbed his head.

"But she's not," Marcus said, "Yin even said so."

"He could be wrong. Who knows what The Storm could do to her." Austin said with sadness and pain in his voice. "Everyone keeps saying sorry, and it keeps putting bad thoughts in my head."

"Look at me, Austin." Austin looked up at Mr. Davidson. "We will get her back, okay? You need to think positively. We have a game plan to get her back."

"No, we don't," Austin said as he stood up to walk around the room. "We have: Let's get the sword, and then we go get Elsie. That is not a plan at all. That's a to-do list."

Olivia ran into the room. "Hey, I heard what happened. Are you okay?" she said as she ran to check on Austin.

"Yeah, I'm fine. I just can't wait until summer. I need to find Elsie now."

"We all want to find her, Austin," Olivia said, "but even you said yourself, we can't go walking right into The Storm's house and have him give her to us."

"But we can." Austin said, "they want me. Trade me for Elsie."

"You are the only person that can stop Storm. We can't just deliver you to him on a silver platter," Marcus said.

Austin started scratching his head. "I don't know what to do then."

"She will be okay," Olivia said as she grabbed Austin's hand.

"I want to believe that," he said as he turned back to her.

Marcus stood up and walked over to Austin. "I need you to be okay. I need you for support at the game tonight."

"I'll be okay," Austin said.

The rest of the day, no one said a word to Austin after they heard what happened. Some students were calling him a freak, and others were scared of him. After school, Austin and Olivia went back to his house. Marcus had to stay behind and warm up for the game. Everyone met at Austin's house.

"This doesn't feel right," Austin said.

"What doesn't?" Olivia asked.

"Us going to a football game when Elsie is missing. I'm going to stay behind to try and find a way to get her back."

Yin walked up to Austin. "I'll see what I can find out. You go to the game and enjoy yourself and support your friend. If I find anything, anything at all. I will come to get you right away. I promise."

Austin nodded his head. He wanted to find Elsie but also wanted to be there and support Marcus. Austin's dad brought his laptop to the game because he wanted to continue his research for anything that could help them. Everyone got in the car and drove to the school for the football game.

A God Among Men

They found their seats right before kickoff. It was a packed house. The first quarter had started. After a few plays from the visiting team, the Silverdale Knights intercepted a pass! now Marcus was able taking the field. Everyone was cheering for him. The ball was snapped and handed off to him. First play of the game, Marcus ran for a big play. Marcus was one of the best running backs in the state. A few drives later, he already had seventy-six yards and a touchdown. We just reached halftime, and the Silverdale Knights were up by seventeen. The halftime kick-off was about to go underway. The visiting team kicked off to the Knights, and Marcus was in the backfield to return the kick. With a few spin moves and a good block, Marcus took it all the way for the touchdown! He was having a great game, and the crowd loved it. Austin, Olivia, and everyone else were having a lot of fun. Everyone forgot about The Storm for a little while. The football game ended, and the Silverdale Knights won the championship 37-14. Marcus won the game MVP. They all decided to go out and get food at the mom-and-pop diner after the game to celebrate.

Across the sea in The Storms throne room. "Humans need a ruler. They need to be commanded and controlled like the animals they are." The Storm said, looking out over the ocean through an endless storm. He turned and started to walk to a pillar in the middle of his throne room.

"You think I'm bad? Humans have killed other humans more than I ever have, and I've killed a lot. Some of them even deserved it, but most of them didn't. And I've enjoyed each and every kill. There is one that I will enjoy more than the rest of them." The Storm knelt down. "And that is when I kill your big brother." he said as he rubbed the back of his finger on Elsie's cheek. She was chained to the pillar, just screaming and crying through the tape over her mouth.

Chapter 8

One Of The Six

Everyone was having a wonderful time out at dinner. They were playing pool. The adults were having drinks. Everyone was making small talk. Although everyone was happy for now, Austin couldn't just sit around while Elsie was gone. Austin stood up from the booth and walked toward the door. His dad saw this and ran after him.

"Where do you think you're going?" Austin's dad asked.

"I can't just sit here drinking milkshakes and laughing while Elsie is still out there somewhere, probably scared." Austin said.

"I understand. But she knows we are looking for her and that we are going to do everything to get her back," his dad said.

"But we're not! Us having dinner at a restaurant isn't looking for her or doing everything we can to get her back! I'll see you guys at home. I'm going to try and find something that can help us."

Austin decided to walk home. It was dark. The only real light was the moonlight and a few streetlights here and there. Austin heard a noise behind him. It sounded like someone had stepped on a stick.

"Who's there?" Austin said as he turned around. All he could hear now was the wind against the trees. He turned back around to continue home. Yin was right in front of him. Austin got startled a little.

"Are you out of your mind?" Yin asked Austin.

"What are you talking about?" Austin asked.

"The Storm has people out to get you. Yang probably has people out to get you. You are walking around with a target in your back and a price tag on your head. You can't be walking around alone at night," Yin said.

Austin could hear the concern in his voice. "Okay, sorry, I wasn't thinking about it like that. I was just going home to see if I could find where Elsie is," Austin said.

"Come with me," Yin said as Austin followed him into the Black Forest. The Black Forest was a very large forest right outside of Silverdale. Many people like camping in the forest, but a few have gone missing. It's called the Black Forest for a reason. Even in the day, with a bright sun in the sky, the forest was still pitch black. It was so dense not even the sunlight can shine through.

"Where are we going? Austin asked.

"I may have found something," Yin said as he continued to walk through the Black Forest.

Austin was trying to keep up. Deep into the woods, Yin walked to a small open area, staying in the shadows at the tree line. He knelt down behind a tree and looked back at Austin.

"We're here," he said as he pointed to an old-looking cabin.

"What is this place?" Austin asked.

"You could call it a safe house. I've been scoping this place out, and I believe some of The Storm's huntsmen use this cabin as a rendezvous point."

"You think Elsie could be in there?" Austin asked as he started to walk toward the cabin.

"No," Yin said, pulling him back into the shadows, "but they might know where to look."

"So why are we just standing here? We should charge in there and get some answers," Austin said as he pushed Yin's hands off him and moved toward the cabin again. Yin grabbed him again and pinned him up against a tree away from the cabin.

"Get off me!" Austin said, trying to push Yin off again.

"Shh," Yin said, putting his hand on Austin's mouth. Yin peeked around the corner and saw a huntsman standing on the porch. The huntsmen turned and walked to the other side. "Be smart about this, Austin. We need a plan. No one in the cabin knows about Elsie. The big man comes every night, the one that had Elsie over his shoulder. We need to wait for him," Yin said, letting go of Austin.

Austin agreed to be quiet and to wait for the large huntsman. As it got later into the night, Austin and Yin just sat in the woods waiting. "Yin, look," Austin said, pointing at a dirt trail leading to the cabin. They saw three pairs of headlights far in the distance. "I may have a plan," Austin said to Yin. He knelt back and started to explain it to Yin.

The huntsmen inside the cabin all went out front to meet the vehicles coming toward them. Austin, staying in the shadows, moved quickly behind the cabin. There was a window that he was able to climb through. The vehicles all pulled up, and the large huntsman got out and ordered the others to unload all the supplies. The light inside the cabin went out.

"Who's still inside? Everyone was supposed to come help unload." the huntsman captain asked.

"No one, sir. We all came out front together. Maybe the candle blew out. Would you like me to go back in and light it?" one of the huntsmen asked.

The captain just nodded his head. He turned back to help unload as the smaller huntsman ran inside. He lit the candle again. The big huntsman saw the light turn back on but went out a second later. With the light not going back on, he decided to go check for himself. He ordered the other men to continue working. Once inside, he looked around, but could not see anything. He took a few steps toward the candle to light it.

"You messed with the wrong family," Austin said, his face glowing from a match.

"The man-god," the huntsman captain said, smiling. "Are you stupid? You just delivered yourself right to me."

"I'm just here to find out where you guys are keeping my little sister."

The large man just laughed. "You must have hit your head. Men, come tie the man-god up!" he yelled over his shoulder to his men outside.

"They won't be joining us tonight," Yin said, leaning on the side of the doorframe of the cabin. The large huntsman turned around quickly to see Yin standing there.

He looked out front and saw all the huntsmen lying on the ground unconscious.

"I see you brought your daddy with you for protection," he said as he turned to Austin.

"I'm not here to protect him," Yin said as he walked in and closed the door behind him. "We need information, and I'm here to make sure he doesn't tear you apart before we get what we want."

Austin stood up and started to walk toward him. "Where's my sister?"

"Dead, hopefully," the large man said with attitude.

"Oh, big mistake," Yin said, laughing as he turned away from him and Austin. Austin pulled his hand back and landed a right hook on the large man. He didn't knock him down but still did some damage causing him to bleed.

"Where is my sister," Austin asked again, this time grabbing a knife off the table. Austin was having a strange look in his eyes. This started to worry Yin.

"You don't scare me, boy. After I deliver you to The Storm, I'll make sure you watch as I kill your sister myself!" the man yelled, slamming his hands on the table. As soon as his hands hit the table, Austin stabbed the knife right into one. The large man screamed in pain. Yin saw Austin's eyes flash black for a second then back to normal. Yin was now keeping a close eye on Austin.

"I don't think you understand what's happening here. You aren't leaving this cabin with air in your lungs. They will be carrying your corpse out of here," Austin said, twisting the knife. The man screamed louder in pain.

"I hope you mean yourself!" he said as he charged a lightning bolt in his hand to throw at Austin.

Yin stepped in and put his hand in front of the lightning bolt. His hand absorbing the lightning. Austin pushed Yin out of the way and pulled the knife out of the huntsman's hand. He kicked the table into the huntsman, knocking him back. Austin threw the knife into the huntsman's shoulder. The huntsman started to pull the knife out, but Austin ran and jumped over the table. He kneed the man in the face and pushed the knife deeper into the man's shoulder.

"I'm going to ask you again," Austin said, pulling the knife out, ripping flesh as it came out. The huntsman screamed in pain. "Where is my sister!?" Austin asked again.

"The Storm has her. When he hears what you did tonight, he might just send you her hand in a box. Hand for a hand." the man said, pointing at the hand that Austin stabbed.

"Oh, he won't hear about tonight," Austin said as he walked out of the cabin, closing the door behind him. Yin walked up to the man. His eyes began to glow, and Yin held his hand out. Austin turned his head and saw a bright white flash coming from inside the cabin. A few seconds later, Yin walked out.

"No one will hear about tonight," Yin said to Austin.

"So how do we get to The Storm? We now know that he definitely has her. Me and you, right now, let's go. Get in and out quickly. We can get her," Austin said.

"Even The Storm isn't dumb enough to let something like that happen. Our best chance is to stick to the original plan," Yin said.

A God Among Men

Austin looked down. "Yeah, you're right." I just wish there was something I could do to get her back now."

Yin was walking back toward the path they started on. Austin lifted his head and saw a faint light in the distance, slowly coming toward them.

"Yin, what is that?" Austin asked as Yin walked back to him to see where he was looking. A hooded person was walking toward them with a walking stick and a lantern to light his way. When the hooded person got to the tree line, they stopped.

"Hello, stranger, nice night for a walk?" Yin yelled over to them. They just turned around and began to walk away.

"What was that about?" Austin asked.

"I think I know who that is," Yin said as he began to walk after them.

"Wait, you know them?" Austin started to walk after Yin.

A mysterious fog started to roll in where they were in the woods. Gusts of wind started to blow. Causing small breaks in the black to let some moonlight shine through. They couldn't see the mysterious person anymore. They were about to give up and go home when they came across another small opening in the trees. The hooded person was standing in the fog, facing away from them.

"Hello?" Yin asked as he walked closer to them. Austin was right behind him, looking around.

Just as soon as Yin reached out to grab the person's shoulder, the cloak, lantern, and walking stick, all collapsed and fell into the fog. Yin reached down and picked up the cloak. "It was a trick. Get behind me."

Before Austin could move, the mystery person came sliding in, tripping Austin with the walking stick. They swung the stick around and smacked Yin in the chest, launching him back into a tree. Austin quickly got up and tried throwing a punch. The hooded figure blocked it with the staff and kicked out Austin's leg, knocking him to a knee. The figure then smacked him across the face, knocking him to the ground. Yin ran to help Austin. The hooded person swung the staff into Yin's stomach. Then they slammed it on his back, knocking him to the ground. Austin tried to get up, but the mystery person kept knocking him down. Yin stood up, and his eyes turned white. He pushed his hand forward, and a beam of light energy came from his hand.

The mystery person used the staff to block Yin's attack. The staff seemed to be absorbing the beam of light. Yin held his other hand out and his staff of light energy formed. Yin spun it around and tried slamming it on the mystery person. They blocked Yin's staff with their own. They spun around and hit Yin on his side, causing a blast of the same light energy to hit Yin, launching him into a nearby tree again. Austin ran up, and the hooded person spun and hit Austin with the staff, and another blast of white light burst from the stick and launched him also into a nearby tree. Both Austin and Yin were unconscious.

When Austin came too, they were in a room made of rock. A cave hidden deep in the woods. Austin started to get up. He was looking around the room and saw the cave was full of paintings and carvings. There was a table in the middle with empty vials scattered everywhere, like a science experiment gone wrong. There were also various pieces of furniture made of wood around the room as if this was someone's home. The paintings and carvings looked to be of the Gods. Austin saw Yin lying on the ground and went over to wake him up. When Yin woke up, he looked around the room also.

"Where are we?" Austin asked.

"I've never seen this place before," Yin responded as he tried to stand up. Austin saw what looked like the hooded person's walking stick leaning on a wall. He walked over and reached to pick it up.

"I wouldn't do that, Austin Kale," said a voice. Austin and Yin were looking around.

"Who are you? How do you know who I am?" Austin said, making fists.

"Put down your hands, Austin. You see how well that worked out for you last time," the voice said. Austin looked at Yin while slowly lowering his hands.

"Where are we?" Yin asked.

"We are nowhere. This place doesn't exist," said the voice.

"Why are we here?" Austin asked.

"Because you need to see," the voice said.

"See? See what?" Austin and Yin saw a shadow of someone standing behind them.

They turned around quickly. Austin threw a punch. The hooded person ducked under the punch and then hit Yin in the chest with his left hand knocking him into the cave wall while landing his right palm on Austin's forehead. Suddenly Austin couldn't move. His eyes rolled back, and he fell to the ground. Austin opened his eyes and stood up to look around. He saw that he was on a planet full of fire and darkness. Buildings were collapsed and burning. Volcanos were erupting in the background, and red and black lightning was striking all around.

"Where am I? Yin?" Austin asked.

"Yin won't be joining you," a voice said.

"Where am I? Where did you take me?" Austin asked again.

"You are on Earth," the voice said.

"Earth? This looks nothing like Earth," Austin said.

"Oh, but it is. This is the Earth you will build. Don't believe me? Let's take a closer look."

Everything around Austin started spinning. When it stopped, he was standing in a large room. He saw steps leading up to two large seats. Men, women, and children were in lines around the outside of the room, chained together around their hands and feet with an iron collar on each one. Austin noticed one of the girls in chains. It was Olivia!

"Olivia!" Austin yelled.

"She can't hear you. Or see you. No one can," the voice said.

"Let her go!" Austin yelled.

"It wasn't me who put her in chains Austin Kale. You did. Watch."

Everything spun around Austin again, and now he was up the steps next to the large thrones. Someone was sitting on one of them. Long black cloak with the hood up. Another person in a black cloak and the hood up was walking up the steps. The person sitting on the thrones got up and walked toward the top of the steps. The other one knelt before the first. The one standing removed their hood. It was Yang!

"What is Yang doing on Earth?" Austin asked.

"You brought her here," the voice said.

"You have served me well," Yang said, speaking to the hooded person. "You knelt before me as a loyal apprentice. Now rise and rule next to me as my king."

The person stood up and removed the hood. It was Austin!

"Wait. That's me. Why am I standing with Yang? Why am I letting all of this happen?" Austin asked the voice.

"Let's show you one more thing," the voice said. Everything spun around one last time. Austin saw himself walking with the black cloak on. Walking past Olivia, who was chained up.

"I hope you're happy, Austin," Olivia said.

"What did you just say to me?" the cloaked Austin asked as he spun around to face Olivia.

"I said I hope you're happy. You got your family killed, and your friend also. You're the reason Elsie died!" She yelled. "You could have stopped all of this. You were supposed to save us."

"What is she talking about?" Austin asked the voice. Austin's eyes rolled back again, and he fell to the floor. When he opened his eyes, he was back in the cave. The hooded person took their hand off Austin's forehead.

"That was some kind of trick, wasn't it?" Austin asked, rubbing his head.

"No trick. That's your future," the person said, walking to a table in the middle of the cave.

"I would never let that happen. Who are you? I want answers!" Austin demanded.

The person slowly took off their hood. It was an older man. His eyes were wrapped with bandages. They looked like they had been on his head for a very long time.

"What happened to your eyes?" Austin asked. Yin looked up and saw the man.

"You?" Yin asked.

"You know him?" Austin asked Yin.

"I know of him. Of them."

"Them?" Austin asked, confused. "What are you talking about, Yin?"

"Of all the years I've been on this Earth, I have never seen them. They are called the Sages of the Gods. He's one of the Six," Yin said, walking closer to Austin.

"There are six of them? Where are the others?" Austin asked.

"Scattered around the globe, forever wandering. Our purpose was to serve the Gods, but when they all abandoned us and the world, we decided to serve the world. When we heard the word of a man-god, we started to believe there was hope. A God that fought for man," the sage said. "But I was wrong. You do not fight for man. You fight for yourself. You are not welcome here."

"Woah, back up a second. I will fight for this world. Who are you to tell me? You don't know me," Austin said.

"Austin Kale of 128 Winter Crest Lane. Son of Brian Kale and Leah Kale. Big brother to Elizabeth Kale and Ava Kale. Your real dad is the God of light, Yin. Senior at Silverdale High School. Born a man-god will grow to destroy us all," the sage said as he turned to Austin. He walked around like he could see perfectly fine. Austin didn't know what to say or how to respond. "Even with both of your eyes, you still see less than I do. There is a darkness growing in you, boy. Your drive for revenge and anger for them taking your sister will cause what you saw the future to be like. Stop fighting for your own selfish reasons and fight for this world," the sage said as he grabbed his staff and held it up to Austin "or so help me, I can end you right here and save the world from that chaos."

Yin tried to step in front of Austin.

"Don't try anything, Yin. You're powerless here," The sage said.

"You have my word," Austin said, stepping back in front of Yin. "I will only fight for this world."

The sage put his staff down and turned to walk back to the table.

"You're wrong, you know. The other Gods might have abandoned this world but not Yin. He fights for it," Austin said to the sage.

"Oh really? So the past seventeen years of destruction and suffering at the hands of The Storm must all be in my head, then? Or all the years before then, with the other Gods causing chaos around the world? And let's not forget Yang, the Goddess of death. Every planet she goes to dies. It's only a matter of time until she reaches this one," the sage replied.

Yin looked down. He started to feel disappointed in himself. "You're right."

Austin looked over to Yin.

"I let the world down. It should have never come this far. I should have stopped it before any of this happened. I am sorry," Yin said.

"Yin, you are stopping Yang right now from coming and destroying the world. We won't let that happen. Me or you. We are in this together," Austin said. He turned to look at the sage. "I did want to ask you, how was it that you were able to stop Yin's power like that when we fought in the woods?"

"Long ago, after the fall of the First Men, a group of six of us found a very large and old tree. We believe it to be the first spot Yin touched when he came to Earth. The staff is made from one of the branches," the sage said, "we have studied the Gods for as long as we can remember."

"Well, what happened to your eyes?" Austin asked.

"The Gods happened. They blinded us to try and make us weaker and submit to their power. When we did not, they scattered us around the world."

"I truly am sorry. I had no idea," Yin said.

"Save it. It's why we stayed hidden all these years. We want nothing to do with the Gods anymore. You two can just get out," the sage said as he pointed to a tunnel.

"Please just listen to us. We are going to fix everything. We have a plan," Austin said.

"Yes, yes, I know. Find the sword and stop The Storm. Save yourself some trouble, boy. Go live a normal life. When this world is destroyed, Yin can just create a new one as his next project." the sage just pointed back at the tunnel. Austin and Yin both walked out of the tunnel leading them into the woods.

"Come on. We need to go tell my family everything that happened," Austin said.

"No, you do. The sage was right. I did abandon this world. I let the other Gods ruin it when I should have held my ground and protected it. I let the world down." Yin turned to Austin and put his hands on Austin's shoulders. "Don't become what you saw. Save this world. Be better than me." Yin turned away in shame, transformed into a raven, and flew off into the moonlight.

Austin just stood there and watched Yin fly off. That didn't change anything. He still needed to tell his family everything that had happened. He looked around and saw multiple trails. He wasn't sure which way to go.

"Austin."

Austin turned around and saw the sage standing at the entrance of the cave. "Yin needs to find his own way. He has been lost for a while. You have been helping him remember who he is. He will be back. You also need to let go of this darkness that you're holding on to. This need for revenge is what will lead you down a path you can't come back from. Winter is almost over. Your real journey is about to begin." The sage pointed down one of the paths "May we meet again."

Austin looked down the path and back to the sage. "Thank you," and he took off running down the path to go back home.

Chapter 9
Face To Face

Across the sea, The Storm sat on his throne. Elsie still chained up to the center pillar, had no more tears left as she stared at the floor. A skinny man with a hood ran into the room and bowed. The Storm allowed him to speak.

"Sir, I went to the safe house after we didn't hear back at the usual time. You were right. There were no survivors." The Storm slammed his fist down, and lightning struck right next to the messenger. The Storm stood up from his throne and walked down the steps right toward Elsie. He knelt down in front of her.

"I think it's time I pay your brother a visit myself." He said, brushing her hair with his hand.

Elsie glared and looked the other way. The Storm stood up and walked to the entrance of his throne room. With the sound of a whistle, two large lions ran out of a dark room and walked right behind him. Elsie started screaming and shaking to try and get out of the chains, but it was no use. All she could do was pray for Austin's safety, and that he would come for her soon.

A God Among Men

Back in Florida, Austin ran all the way home. He had been out all night, and the sun was starting to come up. Through the trees, he could start to see the backs of some of the houses in his neighborhood. Marcus woke up after getting home from a great night out with his friends. He saw Austin running down the street toward his house. Marcus quickly got dressed and ran outside to meet him. Austin was running on the other side of the street, so Marcus ran out of his house to run with Austin. Austin did not see Marcus.

"Hey!" Marcus yelled.

Austin tripped and fell. Marcus startled him.

"Wow, you suck," Marcus said as he helped Austin up. "Why are you running?"

"I'll tell you when we get to my house. Come on." Austin took off running again with Marcus right behind him. There were a few extra cars parked out front of Austin's house. They got to the front door and went right in. Olivia was there and hugged Austin as soon as he got inside the door.

"Are you okay? Where were you?" Olivia asked. Austin's mom and dad hugged him, also.

"Yeah, I'm fine. I was out with Yin," Austin said, pushing his parents off.

"You need to stop scaring us like that. You can't just run off and not tell us where you went. Especially after what we found out about you and what happened to Elsie," his mom said.

"We thought you went after her by yourself," his dad added.

"I wanted to. I wanted to pack my bags and leave you guys a note and get the first flight out, but I can't.

There's something I need to tell you guys. But first, can I get changed?" Austin asked.

"Of course," his mom said.

Austin walked to his room. Once he opened the door, he froze for a second, confused. Someone slept in his bed.

"I hope you don't mind." Austin turned around and saw Olivia right behind him. He didn't even realize she was wearing one of his shirts and his sweatpants until right now.

"When you didn't come home last night, your parents offered to let me stay the night and wait for you. We were all worried, but I knew you would come back. You always do." Austin and Olivia were leaning in for their first kiss...

"Hey, Austin! Where did you go last night?" Marcus said, interrupting them.

Austin let out a big sigh, and Olivia just looked at him with a little smile on her face.

"Oh, my bad, you guys were having a moment. Got it. I'll just go wait in the kitchen." Marcus started to walk away while singing, "Austin and Olivia... Sitting in a tree."

"He's a child," Austin said as he just shook his head and walked into his room to change.

Olivia just laughed and walked back to the living room to wait for Austin to come out. Once he finished changing, he took a second to just stare into the mirror. He was still trying to wrap his mind around everything that happened so far and what is still to come. He blinked, and his reflections had black eyes, just like Yang's. Austin was startled, screamed and took a few steps back which caused him to fall over the chair in his room. Everyone in the living room could hear the thud. Olivia ran back to check on him.

She opened the door just as Austin got back up to look in the mirror. This time his eyes looked normal.

"Everything okay back here?" Olivia asked, looking around the room.

"Yeah, I just tripped and fell, that's all," Austin said, trying to play it off.

"Everyone is waiting for you," Olivia said.

"Right. Let's go," Austin said as he and Olivia walked to the living room. He and Olivia both sat down. Everyone was quiet, just waiting for Austin to speak.

"Last night, I did have every intention to go try and find and rescue Elsie by myself. As I was walking home, Yin found me and took me to a cabin in the woods."

"Wait, where is Yin?" Austin's dad asked.

"He's gone," Austin said.

"Gone? Gone where?" his mom asked.

"I'm not sure, and I have no idea when he or if he will come back," Austin said.

"He does know that summer is right around the corner, right? Which means the summer solstice will be here soon," Mr. Kale said.

"I think we need to prepare for this part of the journey without Yin," Austin said. Everyone was now more worried. Austin continued to tell everyone about the huntsmen in the woods and the sage they found.

"Just when I thought this year couldn't get any weirder, all of this happens," Marcus said.

"So you have darkness in you?" Austin's mom asked, being very concerned. Austin had a small flashback to earlier in his room when he saw his eyes go black.

"Austin?" His mom said, "Are you okay?"

Austin snapped out of it "What? Yeah, I'm fine. No, I don't think I have a darkness in me. The way the sage said it seemed like if I went after Elsie with revenge to get her back, then it might trigger something. I'm not one hundred percent sure, but I need to stick to the original plan that we all talked about."

Everyone was silent, processing all the new information. Austin's parents, especially, now have to worry about the darkness in their son. After everyone else left, Austin and Olivia were hanging out on his bed. They were talking about everything that had happened so far. Olivia mentioned that the Prom was next week.

Austin sat right up. "Prom is next week?" he turned to Olivia, "Oh, I am so sorry I didn't ask you in a special way. I had no idea it was this close."

"It's fine, Austin. You had a lot going on, more than anyone I've ever known. Good thing I already got our tickets, my dress, and a tux for you to wear."

"You did all that? I am so sorry, Olivia. With everything going on, I haven't been here with you like I should have," Austin said, getting upset.

"Don't worry about it. Really. You worry about getting your sister back and The Storm, and I'll worry about everything else," Olivia said.

"You are just the best," Austin said as he leaned in for a kiss. Olivia put her finger on Austin's lips, stopping him.

"Oh, I know I am," she said with a little laugh. She stood up and walked out the door. Just as soon as she got in the hallway, she turned back, "I can't wait to see you in the tux." Olivia left to go home. Austin just laid back in his bed with the biggest smile on his face.

A God Among Men

The next week of school went by fast, and prom night was tonight. All the girls at school were talking about it nonstop. Prom night was the night when all the girls look their best and try to look better than everyone else. The guys just go to hang out with their friends. This year was special. It's the school's two-hundred-year anniversary, and this year's theme was *Dancing Under the Stars*.

Prom was taking place on the football field. There was nothing but clear skies predicted for tonight. Austin was dressed in his black jacket and black pants with a sky-blue vest and a sky-blue bow tie. His dad and mom were taking pictures as Marcus showed up in his tux. It was a red jacket with silver pants, a black vest, and a black bow tie. He had his football jersey number stitched onto the back of his jacket. The color scheme, of course, was that of the Silverdale Knights, the team he led to the state championship. Marcus was going to prom with one of the cheerleaders he had been dating recently. Austin and Marcus will be meeting the girls outside in the football field parking lot for pictures. Austin, Marcus, and Austin's parents got into their car to go to school. Marcus told them his parents were on a business trip, but Marcus wanted to get pictures to send to them.

Austin's parents made sure to get a picture of Austin holding Ava. Marcus and Austin were able to get a few pictures together before Marcus' date showed up. Austin stood back, watching them get their pictures taken. In the middle of the pictures, Marcus's date, Cara, looked across the parking lot "oh wow, she looks beautiful."

Marcus and Austin's parents turned around, with all of them saying how beautiful she looked. Austin turned around and saw Olivia in a beautiful sky-blue dress. Her hair, nails, makeup, everything looked perfect.

Austin walked right up to her. "Wow, I'm speechless. You look stunning." Austin couldn't stop looking at her up and down. Austin was mesmerized.

"Hey, Austin, do you think your parents want some pictures?" she asked.

"Oh yes, of course, absolutely." Austin grabbed her hand, and they walked over together.

After pictures, it was time for the parents to go home and for the students to go onto the football field, where they had a dance floor laid out. What a perfect night! All the students were having the time of their lives. Just as the night was coming to an end, the DJ played a slow song, and the lights around the football field dimmed, and it started to drizzle. None of the students let it ruin their night. They kept on dancing in the rain. Austin, on the other hand, stayed on high alert. He's not a fan of what comes after sudden rain. The lightning in the distance was bright enough to be a small strobe light for the dance floor. After the slow song ended, they went right back into a high-energy song. With the lightning as the strobe light and the thunder as the bass, students will be talking about this prom for the rest of their lives.

Austin thought he heard a loud roar just as soon as thunder crashed through the sky and the rain started to pick up. Olivia knew Austin was getting extremely nervous as he kept looking around. He thought he heard the roar again through the thunder. He ran up to the DJ and tried telling him to turn the music off, but the DJ couldn't hear him. He followed the power cords and unplugged everything. All the students became angry and were yelling at Austin.

"Everyone, just stop for a second!" Austin yelled, putting his hand in the air. This time everyone heard the roar. They all turned to the far side of the football field, where the lights were off, and no one couldn't see anything. To everyone's surprise, two lions were walking toward them, and out of the shadows came a man walking between the lions. Austin's eyes widened as he yelled, "Everyone get back!"

Olivia ran to Austin. "Austin, what's going on?" Austin's hands were shaking as he pointed to the man. He looked back to Olivia "That's him. That's The Storm!" he pointed to The Storm.

"I hear there is a man-god among us!" The Storm said as it continued to rain and thunder. "I'll give you all to the count of one to give him to me, or you all die. My pets are very hungry."

The lions roared at the students, and they all started to scream and panic and turn to run away.

"NO ONE MOVE!" The Storm yelled, and it echoed in the thunder. All the students stopped and turned around. "If anyone runs, my beasts go wild."

"I'm the one you want!" Austin yelled over to The Storm.

"Austin, what are you doing?" Olivia said as she pulled on his arm.

"I'm saving you and everyone. Get everyone to safety." He turned back to The Storm.

"I'm the one you're looking for. Just let everyone else go," Austin said as he was slowly walking toward The Storm.

"Kill him," The Storm said to his pets. The lions roared loudly.

"Austin, run!" Olivia screamed.

The lions started to run toward Austin. Teachers were trying their hardest to get the students off the football field. Police sirens were going off in the distance. Austin took his tuxedo jacket off and rolled up his sleeves. He put his fists up, terrified, not knowing his next move.

Marcus turned around and saw Austin standing on the field facing the lions and The Storm. He turned to run toward the parking lot where his friend's truck was. Back on the field, the lions ran toward Austin extremely fast. One of them was coming right for him. The other was looking to attack Austin from the side. The first lion was getting close. Austin regretted his decision to stay behind. Just as soon as the lion jumped in the air to pounce on Austin, he closed his eyes and shoved his hands and arms up to cover himself. A few seconds went by, Austin opens his eyes. He did not get hit by the lion.

Austin looked up and saw a wall of light energy in front of him. The Storm was not expecting that. The lion just jumped right into the wall. Austin put his hands down and the wall just crumbled in front of him. Austin looked around quickly to see if Yin was there. Sadly, he did not see Yin anywhere. The lion was a little disoriented but still tried to jump at Austin again. This time Austin ducked and waved his hands over him. The lion's claw scratched Austin on his chest, but a strong wind came and carried the lion through the air into the football field's concessions building, crashing through the wall.

Austin did not see the second lion sneaking up on him. The lion ran and pounced, but Marcus came crashing through the fence with a truck. He was able to drive onto the field and ram his truck into the lion as it was in the air. Austin turned around, thanked Marcus, and told him to get out of there as fast as he could. Marcus stepped hard on the gas and drove into the lion one more time before driving off the field. For now, both lions were down for the count.

Austin turned to The Storm. "Let's end this now," he said to himself as he ran up to The Storm. The Storm just tilted his head and smiled. Austin got right up in front of him and threw a punch, but it didn't even faze The Storm. Storm then hit Austin with a devastating kick to the chest, launching him back to the other side of the football field. His body skipped on the ground the whole way back as police cars pulled in the parking lot. Right as Austin crashed into the DJ's booth, The Storm put his hand in the sky and threw down a lightning strike onto Austin, hoping it would be a killing blow. Just before he threw his hand down, a police officer shot The Storm, and the bullet hit his arm. It didn't damage him, but he was able to make the slightest move to make the lightning miss Austin. Marcus and some of the other Silverdale Knights were able to run down and pick him up and carry him to safety. Austin was completely unconscious and was taken to the hospital. He suffered a few broken ribs and a bad concussion.

When he woke up in the hospital, his family was there, with Olivia, Marcus, and Mr. Davidson.

"What happened?" Austin said as he tried to sit up. His ribs were hurting badly.

Olivia stood up, and his mom came over and made him lie back down, "don't try to move," his mom said.

"You broke a few ribs," Olivia added.

"Everyone is very grateful for you, Austin." Mr. Davidson said, "I talked to your other teachers, and, well, you already have passing grades in all your classes, and we decided to keep them as your final grade. You don't have to take any finals. The school is in your debt."

"I don't want any special treatment. I just wanted to make sure everyone was safe," Austin said.

"But why you?" Austin's mom said, getting upset. "Why didn't you try to get to safety like everyone else? I don't want to wait at home every night wondering if my son will come home to me," Mrs. Kale said, fighting through her tears. Mr. Kale hugged her. "I feel the same way, but we both know that's just who he is. Even without his powers, he would still make sure everyone is safe first." He turned and looked at Austin. "Just promise us you will be extra careful, okay?"

"Yeah, dad, I promise. But what happened after I blacked out?"

"Well, both lions were shot and killed by the police. The Storm blew up a few police cars with lightning, killing a few officers, and then as more backup came, he walked back into the shadows," Marcus said.

"Marcus, you saved my life back there," Austin said.

"Well, I couldn't let you have all the fun," he said, chuckling. He turned to Olivia and whispered, "If I ever have an idea like that ever again, stop me."

"The police did a complete sweep of the school grounds and the neighborhoods surrounding, but they couldn't find him anywhere," Mr. Davidson added. "We're just glad you're okay."

A God Among Men

"I don't know if I can go through with our plan," Austin said. "That was him, The Storm, in our own backyard. I figured I could try and end it right then and there. He didn't even flinch when I hit him. And he takes one move and sends me flying and puts me in a hospital." Austin took a short pause. "There's no way I can beat him. Even if we get the sword, there is no way he will ever let me get that close again. He was just playing me. I did exactly what he wanted me to do," Austin said with a deep sadness in his voice.

"We will figure it out," Olivia said, grabbing Austin's hand. "I know we will. Right now, get some rest."

Austin closed his eyes and was able to fall asleep quickly due to some of the medication he was taking. Everyone left to go home. Olivia chose to stay behind and stay with Austin. She made sure to bring a picture of Elsie and put it on the table next to his bed.

The next few nights were not that pleasant. Austin woke up a few times in the middle of the night after having bad dreams. Each dream was the same: Him failing everyone and losing to The Storm or Yang coming to Earth and hurting or killing everyone he loves. He could not get a good night's sleep.

After he was discharged from the hospital, his mom, dad, and little Ava were there to bring him home. Ava smiled so big when she was able to see her big brother. Austin had to keep bandages wrapped around his stomach and chest and had trouble with his book bag when he chose to go back to school. Marcus was there to carry his bag for him. On his first day back to school, right as he walked in, all the students were standing in the hallways clapping for him.

They all welcomed him back and thanked him for what he did.

Meanwhile, Marcus was walking down the hallway, asking people, "remember me? I drove the truck! That was me! I'm the truck guy!"

Austin could only laugh. He was glad to be back at school. Once the first period began, the students only had one thing on their mind, Graduation. Most of the students knew what college they wanted to go to. Marcus and Austin were still deciding. Marcus obviously wants to get a scholarship for football. Olivia had her mind set on going to study marine biology. Austin wanted to go for business management, but now, after this past year, he changed his interest to archaeology. Similar to what Mr. Davidson went to college for. Before they could even think about college, they had one priority, getting Elsie back home safely.

Chapter 10
Graduation

Graduation was right around the corner. All the students at Silverdale High School were trying their hardest to get the best grades they could. Studying for finals, completing extra credit, anything to bump up their grade. Everything had been quiet since prom night. Austin's ribs were healed, and there were just a few bruises still on his chest. He's still not sure how he's going to fight The Storm. His punch didn't even turn his head. It's like nothing happened. Austin had enough on his mind instead of worrying about finals and college. All his classmates had already applied to colleges. Some had already heard back. Olivia was accepted into The University of Miami, which has one of the top Marine Biology programs in the country, and it's close to home.

Marcus received a football scholarship from Penn State. His other two choices were Ohio State and the University of Miami. After touring all three colleges, he chose Penn State because that's where his grandfather went and because his girlfriend will be going to Penn State also. Austin just had too much going on to even think about any of that. Mr. Davidson told him he would write an excellent letter of recommendation for Austin when he figured out where he would like to go. His only focus right now was getting Elsie back and stopping The Storm. Marcus and Olivia already said they aren't even thinking about college until Elsie was home safely.

It had been about two months since they last saw Yin. Austin had been looking around on the internet and reading newspapers from major cities around the U.S., but he had not found anything that could be a sign of him. He kept looking across the street to see if he saw a raven sitting in the house watching over them, just like the years before. He even tried to flip the coin Yin gave him to see if he would show up, but Yin was too smart and knew Austin was not in trouble. It made Austin wonder, why didn't Yin show up when The Storm showed up? Austin just realized something. He knows someone who might know where Yin is. He jumped out of bed and got dressed. The sun wasn't even up yet. He went to the kitchen and wrote a note to his parents that read:

Dad, Mom, I love you. I'll be home before school starts. Ps, I took the truck.

Austin grabbed the keys and went outside. He started the truck and drove off to the woods down a familiar dirt path. Eventually, he pulled up to an old cave deep in the Black Forest. The same cave he and Yin woke up in with the sage.

"Sage, I need your help!" he yelled as he ran inside. "Sage?" Austin ran into the big open room inside the cave where he had the vision. The whole cave was empty. The sage must have known Austin would try to come back.

Austin was trying to think of what he could do now. He walked back out of the cave and got in the truck to drive home. The forest was pitch black other than the headlights of the truck. Not even the moonlight could make it through. Austin figured he was about halfway out of the forest when he heard something.

"You shouldn't have come back."

Austin looked in his rear-view mirror and saw the sage sitting in the back seat. He slammed on his brakes and quickly turned around, but the back seat was empty. Was his mind playing tricks on him? Austin turned to face forward and continued home. Just as he looked up, he saw the sage standing in the headlights in front of the truck. Austin made sure the truck was in park and climbed out, making sure never to take his eyes off the sage. "Where did you go?" Austin asked.

"You should not have come back. The Storm may be watching. He has eyes and ears everywhere," the sage said.

"You knew I would come back with more questions." Austin said. The sage just nodded. "Please, I need to know where Yin is. We need him."

"Yin will come back when he is ready. While he was watching over your family for the past eighteen years, the rest of the world has suffered at the hands of The Storm. Before you were born, when The Storm first came to Earth, Yin did confront him and tried to stop him. The fight didn't last long as Yang came to Earth, but only for a few seconds. Instead of fighting Storm, Yin used his power to cast Yang from the world. This left him vulnerable for The Storm to strike. Yin will never be at full power if he keeps blocking Yang."

Austin listened intently, leaning on the front of his dad's truck.

"After The Storm struck Yin down, Yin vanished. For eighteen years, he's been gone. For eighteen years, The Storm has caused chaos around the world. Yin didn't even try to go back and confront him again. The rest of the world just suffered, and Yin let it happen."

Austin didn't like hearing that. "Yin couldn't go back to face The Storm. You just told me that he isn't at full strength. Yin isn't strong enough to fight any of the Gods. If you didn't give up on him so easily, you would have remembered that. Yin chose to let The Storm stay on Earth in order to stop Yang. That doesn't sound like he gave up. You gave up on him. Yin cares about this world. He wants to protect it."

"I hope you're right, boy. The last time Yin left, he hid for eighteen years on a rooftop across the street from your house. You are on your own in your quest to stop The Storm." The sage put his hand on Austin's shoulder. "Until we meet again." The sage vanished right before Austin's eyes. Austin was still trying to process what the sage said. Yin left two months ago and didn't let Austin know when he was coming back or if he was coming back at all.

Austin got back in his dad's truck and drove home. The sun was starting to rise right as Austin got inside his house. He was back before anyone else was awake, and he got ready for school. It was finals week at school. Even though Austin was excused from finals for what he did at prom, he still studied with Marcus and Olivia. While they were studying at school, Austin told Marcus and Olivia what had happened last night.

"Do you think Yin will come back?" Olivia asked.

"I'm not sure now. At first, I didn't doubt it at all, but now I think I might have to do this without him," Austin said.

"Okay, but he left last time because he was hurt. This time he just left to leave?" Marcus asked.

"I wish I knew that answer. I've been staying up night after night reading news articles to see if I could find anything that might be Yin using his power, but it's just hurricane after hurricane. It's almost like The Storm knows Yin left and is attacking now or trying to block me from finding him. My only hope is that The Storm doesn't know our plan to get Aggon's Sword," Austin said as he rubbed his head.

"Not a chance. We will get that sword and go beat The Storm, and then everything will go back to normal, right?" Marcus asked.

"Yeah, I hope so. I just want to have a normal life," Austin said as he started to pack up his things. "I have to talk to Mr. Davidson."

Austin walked to Mr. Davidson's room. Mr. Davidson was looking at a book at his desk. "What's that?" Austin asked.

"Oh, nothing, just a book I'm learning for a class next year. What's going on with you? Ready to graduate?" Mr. Davidson asked Austin.

"Yes and no. Yes, because I'm ready to be done with high school. No, because college is a whole different animal, and I'm nervous about our plan for this summer."

"Well, I would be concerned if you weren't nervous. It's a lot of weight on your shoulders. You have people that want to come and take this adventure with you and help you every step of the way. You just can't lose your cool when we find Elsie. You need to stick to your plan. If you don't, we could lose everything," Mr. Davidson said.

"I am glad I'm going to have all of you there with me," Austin said as the bell rang for the first finals to start.

Austin went to study hall since he didn't have to take the finals, but he wasn't relaxing. He was working hard trying to find any helpful tips about his trip this summer. That's where Austin stayed for the rest of the day and the following day for the rest of the finals. After finals were all finished, Austin, Marcus, and Olivia were about to walk out the front door when Mr. Davidson stopped them.

"Well, I know I'm not supposed to say yet, but you two did wonderful on your finals," he said, looking at Marcus and Olivia. "Next time I see the three of you, you will be walking across the stage at graduation. Get a good night's sleep and enjoy the day off tomorrow, okay? Graduation is a big day, and we have an even bigger summer."

They all said bye to Mr. Davidson and went back to their houses. Austin slept for most of the next day because of his late nights doing research. During the senior's day off, Austin's dad went to the school to sit down with Mr. Davidson and the principal. They were talking about adding extra security, especially after what happened at prom.

The next morning, Austin woke up excited to graduate. He kept thinking that something was going to go wrong, but he was hoping for the best. He got to school with Marcus and met up with Olivia. The rest of their class was waiting outside to get on the school bus to take them to the local college where the graduation was held.

Once they got there, the students went to private rooms, put on their gowns, and prepared for one of the biggest days of their lives. The students heard the music starting to play. Everyone got in line and walked out into a big auditorium. All the students' parents and grandparents were sitting in the audience, clapping and cheering. Once everyone got to their seats, the school choir sang a few songs, and the principal and some teachers talked about the past year of school. Austin looked around and saw three security guards at each entrance and a few stationed with the audience. One by one, the students were called up and walked across the stage. Each one received their diploma and sat back in their seats. The valedictorian came up and gave her speech and led the students in the turning of the tassel. Once high school students, now high school graduates.

After the ceremony, everyone was outside in the courtyard taking pictures. Austin got his picture with Olivia and then one with Marcus. Then the three of them wanted a picture together to keep with them wherever they went. The teachers and principal came out and wanted to get one big class picture. All the students took their caps and threw them in the air. It was picture-perfect. The school year was now officially done. The summer and an important adventure are about to begin.

Chapter 11

Flight 815

The summer had just started. Austin, Marcus, and Olivia would normally be planning vacations with their families, preparing for summer jobs, and getting ready for college. Except, life threw them a curve ball. This whole past year had been a wild roller coaster ride. Everything that had happened so far was nothing compared to what was about to come. Austin had everyone come over to his house to figure out a plan. Who was all going? When are they going? Where are they going? They all sat down around the table. When Austin's dad asked who was going on the trip, Marcus, Olivia, Mr. Davidson, Austin, and himself all raised their hands. That was the easy question. Next, when are they going?

"We can't go the day of the summer solstice. That's playing too close. It has to be a few days before," Austin said.

"Okay, the summer solstice is June twenty-first. We can get on a flight to Egypt a few days before. We can map out where we need to go when we get there," his dad said, "Don't worry about plane tickets. I'll take care of everything. We'll be leaving from the Miami International Airport to the Alexandria, Egypt airport. I'll also take care of hotel arraigments."

"Thanks, Mr. K," Marcus said.

"Yeah, thank you so much," Olivia said.

Austin, Marcus, and Olivia all went outside, and Mr. Davidson stayed inside with Mr. Kale.

"I can't believe it's this close. It's only three weeks away. I still have no idea what I'm going to do when I see The Storm again." Austin said.

"Don't worry. I'm sure you won't get sent to the hospital again," Marcus said.
Austin and Olivia just looked at him.

"What? I'm saying I'm sure you won't go to the hospital again. Meaning you'll win. That's a good thing."

"Does The Storm know what you're trying to do?" Olivia asked.

"I don't think so. I think he believes the sword is destroyed," Austin said.

The three of them heard the front door open. They all turned around and saw Mr. Davidson coming out. He walked up to them, "The next few weeks will fly by. Don't waste them. I understand what we have to do but still enjoy your summer. Go get summer jobs and do whatever will help keep your minds busy until we leave. Okay?" The three of them all agreed.

Mr. Davidson wasn't kidding. The next three weeks flew by. Austin, Marcus, and Olivia all had summer jobs. Their employers knew they had to take a small break. They would meet up in Austin's backyard around his bonfire every night. At first, they would sit around talking and laughing. As it got closer to their trip, the talking and laughter died down. Eventually, it got to the point where no one spoke at all, not even a hello when they came over. They just walked out back and sat around the fire for an hour or two, then got up and left to go home. Not even a peep. They all knew the risks, though no one wanted to talk about it. Austin thought about it more than anyone. It might be a one-way trip for him. If he failed, he would not come home, maybe no one would.

The morning of the trip, Austin made sure to get up early and make his mom breakfast. He made sure to give her the biggest hug and kiss, and did everything his mom asked without question. They booked a nighttime flight so they would land in the morning.

"You come home to me, Austin Kale," she said.

"I will, mom, I promise," he said as he and his dad walked out the door, knowing he might not be able to keep that promise.

Austin and his dad got into the truck, and they went to pick everyone up. Austin, Marcus, and Olivia all sat in the back seat, and Mr. Kale and Mr. Davidson sat in the front seat.

No one talked on the car ride there. They just listened to the music on the radio. Each one looked out the windows.

"I know we are all thinking the same thing. But we can't be thinking like that at all. We need to think positively. This plan will work," Austin's dad said.

Austin put his hand on his dad's shoulder, "Thanks, dad," Austin said with a smile. His dad just smiled back.

Once they got to the airport, everyone got out of the truck and grabbed their suitcase from the bed. They walked into the airport and right up to luggage drop-off. Each of them had a carry-on bag as well. It would be a long flight. They had their phones to watch movies and headphones to listen to music. Olivia and Mr. Davidson both had books. Mr. Kale had a neck pillow. He was going to try and sleep the whole flight. They were walking through the airport, trying to find the terminal. Once they found it, they all sat down and looked out the window at the airplanes. Austin's dad told him about how, when he was little, he wanted to be a pilot.

"Why didn't you?" Austin asked.

"I also wanted a family. And if I was a pilot, I would be away from you guys for little bits at a time."

"Well, I'm glad you are here with me now, dad. I wouldn't want anyone else coming with me." Austin gave his dad a hug.

"Well, we have about an hour to kill, so why don't you guys go get a snack or something," Mr. Kale said to Austin, Marcus, and Olivia. He gave them some money, and they went to get snacks. Mr. Kale and Mr. Davidson just hung out at the terminal. Austin, Marcus, and Olivia were all walking around the airport, looking at the different little shops they had. Each one got a bag of food.

"Flight 815, prepare for boarding," a voice said over the intercom.

"Come on, that's us," Olivia said. Austin and Olivia turned to walk to their terminal. Marcus almost choked on his food when he heard the voice on the loudspeaker.

"Uhm, what? Guys?" Marcus was trying to get their attention. He ran after them. Once they all got to the terminal, Marcus looked like he saw a ghost. "Guys, what

- 134 -

did you say our flight was? The flight number?" Marcus asked.

"Flight 815," Austin said looking at his ticket.

"We have to change our flight. We can't get on this plane."

"What are you talking about?" Olivia asked. Austin, his dad, Olivia, and Mr. Davidson we're all looking at Marcus, confused.

"Flight 815. Seriously? None of you are worried? That TV show. A plane crashed on a mysterious island with a monster in the woods. Their plane was also Flight 815. We can't get on that plane," Marcus said nervously.

Everyone just smiled and thought it was funny. Austin put his arm around Marcus. "That was just a TV show. None of that was real," Austin said.

"Coming from the kid who just found out he's a God," Marcus said, pushing Austin's arm off him. "I'm telling you now, something bad is going to happen on this flight."

"I'll tell you what, if anything happens, I'll make sure to save you first," Austin said with a little laugh.

There were about thirty more minutes until the passengers could start boarding. Olivia was reading her book. It was about some kid with a lightning bolt on his forehead. She thought it was very interesting. Marcus was playing on his phone trying not to worry about the flight. Austin was just looking out the window watching the planes take off. Mr. Davidson was reading the newspaper, and Mr. Kale was resting his eyes. Before they knew it, the announcement came on the loudspeaker:

Flight 815 is now boarding.

A God Among Men

Everyone grabbed their bags and packed up whatever they were using until they got on the plane. Austin and Olivia were sitting next to each other, and Marcus was sitting right behind them. Austin's dad and Mr. Davidson were sitting across from the kids. Olivia began to read her book again. Marcus was back on his phone. Everyone was back to what they were doing before getting on the plane. Austin was watching everyone else board the plane and take their seats. Austin had the window cover shut because he was going to try and sleep for a little bit on the plane. Out of nowhere, Austin heard what sounded like tapping on the roof of the plane. A lot of tapping. Marcus took his headphones out.

"What is that?" he asked.

"I'm not sure," Austin said.

"Attention everyone," one of the flight attendants said over the plane's speakers, "The flight has been delayed due to unexpected severe weather."

Austin quickly opened the window cover, and it was pouring outside. Lightning started striking, and thunder was crashing in the clouds. Austin turned around to look at his dad. What are they going to do now?

"Do you think The Storm is here?" Olivia asked.

"I don't know. Maybe he's just trying to stop us? But how? I didn't think he knew what our plan was," Austin said. He looked back out the window. Lightning was striking all around. It even struck the airport, causing part of it to lose power as well as some nearby planes. They all shut off, including the plane Austin was on. The backup generators were able to get the airport power back on right away, but the planes were still down.

"We need to get off this plane. We need to find another way to get to Egypt," Austin said as they all stood up. Right before they started to walk to the door, the plane shook. It felt like something had fallen or landed on the wing of the plane. Olivia got back in her seat and looked out the window. Austin looked out the window leaning over her.

"What is that?" she asked.

"It's a man," Austin said.

All the other passengers looked out of their windows also. A man was kneeling on the wing of the plane in a white cloak with the hood up. He stood up as lightning was coming right for him. He took his hood down and looked back at the window Austin and Olivia were looking out. It was Yin! Yin's eyes lit up bright white. Yin put his hand in the air. The lightning hit his hand, and he pointed his other hand back to the sky, away from the plane and the airport, redirecting the lightning away. A gust of wind blew hard, he put his hand out, and the wind stopped. A few times, lightning tried striking him down, and each time he redirected it. Austin could not believe what he was seeing. It was poetry in motion. Yin's movements were so smooth it looked like he was dancing on the wing. Redirecting lightning, calming the winds when they picked up and slowing the rain. He even stopped a tornado from touching down by spinning the air in the opposite direction toward it. He was battling what would have been a disaster. He was battling the hurricane itself. When Yin had an opening, he slammed his palm onto the wing of the plane. The plane's lights and engine all turned back on.

A God Among Men

Austin stood up, "Everyone, please take your seats and buckle up. We are getting out of here." Austin went up to the flight attendant. "We need to take off now," he said.

"We can't. The weather is too bad outside," she said.

"Then I need to talk to your pilot," Austin said.

"I'm sorry, that's not possible." she said back.

Mr. Kale walked up behind Austin. "Can you just tell the pilot that Brian Kale wants to say hi?"

The flight attendant just looked at both of them. She rolled her eyes and turned to grab the pilot's phone to call and ask him.

Austin turned to his dad with a confused look on his face. "I told you I wanted to be a pilot. I went to school for it. I just never finished because your mom got pregnant with you."

The pilot came out of the cockpit. He saw Mr. Kale and his eyes opened wide. "Brian!" he said and gave him a big hug. "What are you doing here? The weather is crazy."

"We don't have a lot of time, so listen well. This hurricane was sent by the God, Storm. He's trying to stop us. There is another God on the wing of your plane fighting the hurricane. We need to take off now!" Mr. Kale said. The pilot just looked at both of them like they were crazy.

"Trust me," Mr. Kale said.

"I wish I could, but I haven't gotten the clearance to take off."

Austin grabbed the pilot's shoulders. "Take off now! Lives are at stake!"

"You really are your dad's son."

The pilot turned and whispered into the attendant's ear.

Kyle Hodge

"Take your seats. We will take off soon," the pilot said to Austin and Mr. Kale.

The flight attendant told everyone to buckle up and stay seated. Austin grabbed the phone from the attendant "Hello, my name is Austin Kale. I know you all are going to have some questions. But everything will be okay. The flight will be bumpy in the beginning, but I promise you, we will all be safe." He handed the phone back and went back to his seat.

Marcus leaned forward. "You mean that? We're going to be safe getting through this hurricane?"

"I have no idea. We might end up on a mysterious island with a monster," Austin said.

Marcus swallowed his gum. "Now I'm scared. Good job." Marcus sat back in his seat.

Austin looked out the window at Yin. Yin gave a thumbs up, and Austin gave one back. Yin grabbed on as the plane taxied its way to the runway. Yin's eyes lit up again, and he shot a beam of light into the clouds in front of the plane. A hole in the clouds opened to clear skies. The plane just had to make it there, and they would be safe. The plane took off. Yin was still on the wing making sure lightning didn't touch the plane. The wind continued to shake the plane.

"We are all going to die," Marcus said, holding on tight with his eyes shut.

Yin jumped to the other wing of the plane and redirected lightning. They were almost through the hurricane to clear skies. Yin saw lightning about to hit the tip of the plane. He transformed into a raven and flew in front of the plane. He spun around and smacked the lightning with his wing hitting it back into the sky. They made it through the hurricane. About ten minutes later the rain died down to just a little drizzle. The Storm failed to stop them from taking off. Yin was back, and things were looking up for Austin and the group. Austin looked out the window and saw the raven flying next to the plane.

Austin smiled and turned to Olivia and Marcus. "Everything is going to be okay."

The rest of the flight was quiet. Austin had questions for Yin. Where did he go? Why didn't he come back sooner? Did he know The Storm came to his school? Maybe these questions will get answered, or maybe Austin won't ask at all. Austin looked at Olivia. She was just reading her book. He looked back at Marcus. He was still worried they would end up on an island, but he was watching videos on his phone. Austin looked over to his dad, who was sleeping, and then to Mr. Davidson, who had just finished his newspaper and turned the overhead light out to try and get some sleep.

Austin looked back out the window. The sky above was just as dark as the water below. The stars in the sky and the moon were shining bright with the reflection bouncing off the water. He looked back up at Yin with the moon right behind him. For the first time in a long time, Austin felt safe. He felt he could finally get a good night's sleep. He knew Yin was right there to protect him and watch over him just like he had for many years. Austin closed his eyes and went to sleep. Hoping they would be in the beautiful city of Alexandria when he woke up.

Chapter 12
Alexandria

"So, your brother is flying to Egypt." The Storm said, walking over to Elsie. Elsie was dirty and weak. She had cuts and bruises all over her face, arms and legs. She had no strength at all to even scream anymore. At some point, she begged Storm to kill her and end the pain he's caused. He refused as he needs her alive for two reasons. He's trying to use her as bait and as insurance to make sure Austin or Yin don't try anything reckless. As long as Elsie was alive, Storm called the shots. He got close to Elsie, "Come on, scream. Scream for help. Scream for your brother." Storm paused, "I miss the screams. You scream, and then you cry because you know it's pointless. No one is coming for you." Storm stood back up and began to turn and walk away.

"My brother will come for me, and he's going to kill you," Elsie said in a weak voice.

He turned back around. "Oh, I do hope he tries," The Storm said with a smile. "I'll give you a front-row seat for when I kill your big brother. That might be sooner than you think. He was just at the airport. Maybe coming to save you. Or maybe, he's running away because he knows he will fail," The Storm started to laugh. "He is looking for something, something that has been lost for centuries. His last hope is based on an old story. The Sword of Aggon. He will only find disappointment. I watched Yang destroy that weapon myself. Aggon begged for his life, and the great Yin did nothing about it." The Storm looked at Elsie. "Once I kill your brother, I'll kill Yin, and I'll let Yang come deal with you."

On the airplane.

"Austin."
"Get up."
"Austin, wake up."

Austin opened his eyes to Olivia shaking his arm, trying to wake him up. "I'm up, I'm up. What happened? Where are we?" Austin had one of the best periods of sleep he had in a long time. He wiped the drool off his cheek while he was still trying to figure out what day it was.

"Austin, look," Olivia said, as she pointed out the plane window. Austin turned his head and looked out the window. The plane was just about to land, but out in the distance he could see the beautiful and historic city of Alexandria.

"We made it," Austin said. He turned back to Olivia, "What day is it? We didn't miss it, right? I'm not sure how the time change works."

"Relax, we didn't miss it. We still have two days until the solstice. We just need to get to the hotel and maybe do some sightseeing while we wait."

Austin leaned over his seat and lightly smacked Marcus to wake him up. Marcus dropped everything he was holding as he freaked out while waking up. "I'm awake!" he yelled. "Are we here yet?"

"Yeah, look" Austin opened his window cover, and Marcus saw the city.

"It looks old," he said with not much excitement.

"Of course, it's old. The city was founded over two thousand five hundred years ago. It was named after Alexander the Great," Mr. Davidson said to Austin, Marcus, and Olivia.

"Yeah, we are going to need your brain, Mr. Davidson," Marcus said to him.

Everyone waited patiently in their seats until they were able to exit the plane. They needed to get used to the time change. They all got off the plane and went right to baggage claim. About an hour went by until they were all able to get their luggage.

"This way, everyone," Mr. Kale said, waving everyone to follow him. There was a man in a tuxedo waiting for them holding a sign that said "Kale."

Austin went to his dad. "We need to find Yin."

"Okay, we need to go outside to get to the car anyway. Maybe he will be outside."

They all followed the man in the tuxedo. He would be their chauffeur to the hotel. He had a large SUV waiting outside, and he began loading the bags into the car. Austin looked around for Yin. Eventually, he saw a man wearing a white cloak, just like Yin on the wing of the plane. He ran up to him and grabbed his arm. Yin turned around.

"I'm glad I found you. I forgot you weren't inside the plane with us," Austin said with a little laugh.

"Quiet, who all did you tell about your trip to come here?" Yin asked.

"I... I don't know. I guess some people knew," Austin replied.

"You need to be more careful. It wasn't just a coincidence that The Storm sent a hurricane to the airport. Someone tipped him off. Someone told him where you were going to be and at what time," Yin said quietly.

Austin looked so confused, trying to think of who it could be.

"Austin! Yin! Time to go!" Mr. Kale yelled over to them.

Everyone got back to the SUV. One by one, they got in and drove to the hotel. "Dad, the lighthouse is in the opposite direction," Austin said.

"Relax, Austin, we have two more days, and you'll like where we are going."

They pulled up outside of a hotel called Pyramids Eyes Hotel. They went to their rooms, and Austin looked out the window and saw the Great Pyramids of Giza. Austin was amazed at the sight of them. They were more beautiful than he had imagined.

Once everyone was settled, they met down in the lobby. Austin's dad had a tour set up for them. They all seemed pretty excited about it. The tour took them around the three pyramids of Giza. The first was The Great Pyramid of Giza. For over three thousand years, it stood as the tallest man-made structure until 1889 when the Eiffel Tower was completed in France. The pyramid became a tomb for King Khufu, who ruled during the twenty-year span it took to build the pyramid. To this day, there are still mysteries being discovered about the pyramids. Everyone on the tour were taking pictures and videos. Austin noticed something when he looked at the Great Pyramid. He saw a person standing on the pyramid with a tan cloak. The hood was covering their face so he couldn't see it.

"Austin, you okay?" Olivia asked.

Austin turned to look at Olivia "Yeah, I..." he turned back, but the person was gone. "I thought I saw something."

The next stop was the second tallest of the three. Pyramid of Khafre. Built as the tomb of King Khafre. Lastly, the Pyramid of Menkaure. Just like the other two, this one served as a tomb for King Menkaure. There were just so many facts they heard from the tour guide that Austin started getting them mixed up. Either way, he and everyone else were all having a great time. For the rest of the tour, Austin kept having a feeling that someone was following them or watching them.

They visited the Sphinx and a few smaller pyramids next to the largest, called The Pyramids of the Queens. The tour took up most of the day, but it was jam-packed with information and history. Austin loved it. After the tour, everyone went out for dinner and tried coming up with a game plan for the solstice.

"Do you have any idea when we are supposed to be at the lighthouse?" Olivia asked.

"I have no idea," Austin said.

"What are we even looking for?" Mr. Davidson asked.

"I don't know that either," Austin said. Everyone looked confused and concerned. "listen, I wasn't handed directions on how to do any of this. I know I don't have a lot of information."

A God Among Men

"That's no info at all," Marcus interrupted.

"But," Austin said, looking right at Marcus, "We will know it when we see it. I'm sure of it," Austin finished.

"Whatever you say, I'm not going to argue with a God," Marcus said in a sarcastic voice as he drank some of his soda. His eyes widened. "Wait!"

"What is it?!" everyone asked in a worried voice.

"What's the drinking age in Egypt? Can I get a beer?" Marcus asked.

"You still have to be twenty-one to drink here," Mr. Davidson replied, shaking his head. Austin and Olivia just laughed. Austin looked up across the room and saw the same person standing with the tan cloak. Austin didn't take his eyes off him. He stood up and walked toward him.

"Austin, where are you going?" his dad asked, but Austin ignored him. The person with the cloak turned and walked out of the restaurant and went around the corner. Austin got outside and turned the corner, but no one was there. Everyone else came out after him.

"Austin, what's going on?" Olivia asked, "First on tour you were acting weird, and now this."

"I keep seeing someone wearing a tan robe or cloak. It's like they are following us," Austin said.

"I feel it, too," Yin said, standing behind the group. He was leaning on the wall of the restaurant. Everyone turned to look at him. Yin looked up at everyone, "We are not alone here."

"Why can't things be easy for once?" Marcus asked, "It's always something."

After dinner, they all went back to their rooms for the night. Austin and Marcus shared a room, Austin's dad and Mr. Davidson shared a room, and Olivia had her own.

"You really think someone is out there watching us? What if they are looking for the sword also?" Marcus asked.

"The Storm has eyes and ears everywhere," Austin said.

They heard a knock on their door. Marcus rolled off the bed and peaked his head up to look at the door. Austin got up to answer it. It was Olivia. She came in and saw Marcus.

"Hiding?" she asked.

"What? No?... I - I dropped my phone," Marcus said quickly as he stood up.

They heard another knock. Marcus dropped to the floor again. Mr. Kale and Mr. Davidson were at the door. They wanted to check in on everyone.

Marcus stood up, "Phone keeps falling."
Olivia just shook her head.

"I'm glad everyone is here. There's something I need to tell you," Austin said. "After we landed, I found Yin and he told me something... He said that someone told The Storm that we were coming to Egypt and what we're looking for. We all need to be extra careful with what we say to people."

Everyone agreed. The next day they got a ride to the city of Alexandria. They spent all day there. They explored the beach and the shops and even went to the museum. While walking around the museum, Austin came across a feather in a glass case. There was a description next to it. It described a great fire in the year 48 BC. Austin and Olivia read the description and called Yin over to see it.

"What is it, Austin?" Yin asked.

A God Among Men

"Look at this." Austin began to read the description.

The city of Alexandria. The capital of Knowledge and Learning. Home of the great Library of Alexandria. In the year 48 BC, there was a great fire that burned the library and everything inside to ash. All that remained was a single feather. A single raven feather. This is all that remains of the Library of Alexandria.

"Do you know anything about this? Maybe it was a feather of yours from long ago?" Austin asked.

"I have no idea. I don't remember a library or a fire," Yin said as he stared at the feather. He had a weird look on his face.

"Everything okay?" Olivia asked.

"I'm not sure. I feel it calling out to me. Trying to tell me something or remind me of something," Yin said.

"Well, whatever that is, we will figure that out while we're here," Austin said.

They continued exploring the museum. Eventually they walked past a wing of the museum that was roped off. All the lights were off except for one. The one light was shining on a painting. The painting was the only thing in a big empty wing of the museum. Austin turned to one of the workers in the museum.

"Why is this part of the museum blocked off?" Austin asked.

"It was never completed. The project manager in charge of finishing it mysteriously passed away. The same thing happened with the two previous managers. That painting is cursed. Ever since the last manager passed away, no one has entered that room. Have a good day." the worker walked away.

"Well, that's a good reason to go in there," Marcus said sarcastically.

"Yin, do you feel that?" Austin asked.

"Yes, Austin, that painting is calling out to us," Yin said.

"We need to get in there," Austin said, turning to Olivia and Marcus.

"Why us?" Marcus said.

"Come on," Olivia said, grabbing Marcus's arm.

Marcus and Olivia started to walk toward the entrance. They saw a fire alarm. Marcus stood guard, looking for workers and security. Olivia pulled the alarm. The siren started going off all through the museum. Security started getting everyone out of the building, and once the coast was clear, Austin and Yin stepped over the rope and started to walk toward the painting. Halfway through the room, dust and dirt started spinning around right in front of them. Austin and Yin put their arms up to cover their faces. When the dust and dirt cleared, someone was standing there. The room was dark, so it was hard to see.

"Show yourself!" Yin demanded.

"Don't you recognize me… brother?" They stepped into the light. It was Yang! Yang charged at them. Yin stepped in front of Austin and put his hand out. His eyes turned white, and a beam of light came out of his hand and shot at Yang. Yang turned to black smoke and faded into the air. Yin's eyes went back to normal.

"That was Yang?!" Austin asked.

"No. That was just a curse by Yang. She must have somehow placed a curse on this room for anyone who enters. That explains the manager passing away. It was Yang. The only question is, why?" Yin said.

"Let's go find out," Austin said. They went up to the painting. It was of a man standing in the middle of a fire. The man's eyes were glowing white.

"There's no description," Yin said.

"Yin, that looks like you!" Austin said, looking at the picture.

"But what does it mean? I don't remember being in a fire," Yin said seemingly confused.

"We will figure it out. But there has to be a good reason Yang was protecting this painting. It has to mean something," Austin said. They turned to leave the abandoned wing of the museum.

A security guard found them once they walked around the corner "You two! What are you doing still inside?"

"We got lost. We didn't know where the exit was," Austin said as they were escorted to the exit.

Austin and Yin saw Olivia and Marcus and walked over to them.

"So, what was it?" Olivia asked.

"It was a painting of what we think is Yin, standing in the middle of a fire. Yang was protecting the painting. When we walked to it, a spirit of Yang appeared and tried killing us just like the previous managers. Yin stopped her," Austin said.

"So, Yang was killing anyone who got close to the painting. That explains the managers dying. It had to have been painted by someone. Maybe they would have some answers," Olivia said.

"Good idea. We should try and find out who painted the picture," Austin said.

Marcus was oddly quiet during the conversation.

"You okay?" Austin asked.

"Yeah, I just don't like the whole spirit and chasing evil thing. I'm sure I'll get over it," Marcus said.

"We will be fine," Austin said, putting his hand on his shoulder.

Mr. Kale met up with them. "You all ready to go? The sun is already down, and it's a two-and-a-half-hour drive to the hotel. Let's go get some sleep. We have a big day tomorrow."

Everyone made it back to the hotel and in their rooms for the night. Everyone fell asleep quickly except for Austin. He couldn't sleep knowing that if they failed, the world might be destroyed by The Storm. This was their only shot at this. This plan cannot fail, no matter what. Austin was eventually able to fall asleep. The next day, they will head to the lighthouse.

Chapter 13
Lighthouse

The next morning took forever to come. Austin tossed and turned all night, only getting a few hours of sleep. Marcus was snoring, which woke Austin up in the middle of the night. Austin got up, sat out on the balcony and watched the sunrise. He hadn't forgotten about his sister.

"Don't worry, Elsie. I'm coming for you," he said to himself.

A raven flew and landed on his room balcony and transformed into Yin. "Is everything alright?" Yin asked.

"I'm just picturing what Elsie has been through, and it's all because I couldn't protect her," Austin said.

"She's a brave girl, Austin. Strong too. She's lucky to have you as a brother," Yin said. "She will be okay."

There was a knock on the door. Austin walked back into the room. Yin followed him. Austin picked up a pillow from his bed and threw it at Marcus to wake him up. Austin then went to answer the door. It was Olivia, Mr. Davidson, and Mr. Kale. They all walked into the room. Marcus rolled over and saw everyone.

"Uhh, hi, everyone. Of all the things I want to wake up to, this is not on the list," Marcus said as he rubbed his eyes, yawned, and stretched. "Why are we up so early?" he asked.

"Alexandria and the lighthouse are two and a half hours away. We can't miss anything. We need to be there all day if we are going to find what we're looking for," Olivia said.

"Right, right, right, and we don't know what we are looking for or when to look for it. Great plan," Marcus added. He got out of bed and put a shirt on. "Can we at least get breakfast first?" Marcus asked.

"They have breakfast down in the lobby," Mr. Davidson said.

Everyone packed their bags and proceeded down to the lobby. They had a little breakfast bar set up for the guests. One by one, they each got in line and picked what they wanted to eat. They found a table to sit at and had conversations about college and plans after high school. Once everyone was done eating, they went outside and got in the car. Austin took a deep breath.

"You okay?" Olivia asked him.

"I'm just nervous we're going to miss it," he said.

"We will find it. We won't leave until we do," Olivia said as she put her arm around him.

The car started to move. They were on their way to Alexandria. Austin sat quietly, looking out the window. Olivia would look over at him occasionally. Marcus had his headphones on listening to music. About an hour into the drive, Austin's dad slammed on the brakes. Everyone's heads flung forward.

"Is everyone okay?" Mr. Kale asked.

"Dad, what's going on?" Austin asked.

"Look," Austin's dad was pointing out the front windshield. There was a man standing in the road with a tan cloak on, hood up, and holding a staff. He was facing the car.

"Run him over," Marcus said under his breath. Everyone turned and looked at him. "What? Don't we have somewhere to be?" Marcus added.

"Stay in the car," Yin said as he and Austin got out and walked to the front of the car. They both had their hands up, blocking the sun from their eyes.

"Hello there, friend," Yin said.

"Do you need help?" Austin added.

The man was just standing there.

"Listen, we have somewhere we need to be. We don't have time for this. Either tell us what you want, or we will be on our way," Austin said.

The man was still quiet, just standing there.

"Let's just get back in the car. We will go around him," Austin said as he and Yin turned around to get back in the car. Just before he got in, Yin looked at the man again. Yin turned his head and climbed into the car. Mr. Kale turned the wheel. He started to drive the car around the man standing in the road. Just as the car was next to the man, he hit the back end of the car with his staff, and the whole car spun and was once again facing the man. The car's engine shut off completely. Austin's dad tried turning the key...but nothing happened. The man slowly started walking toward the vehicle. Yin and Austin jumped out. They ran in front of the car. Yin held his arm out in front of Austin.

"Wait. I think you know who he is," Yin said. Austin just looked at him.

"You're a sage, aren't you? One of the six?" Yin asked.

The man stopped walking. Held his staff up in the air and struck the ground with the bottom of the staff. Once it hit the ground, a cloud of sand surrounded Austin, Yin, and the car, with everyone inside. When the sand faded away, they weren't on the road anymore. They were in an Egyptian temple. Mr. Kale, Mr. Davidson, Marcus, and Olivia all got out of the car.

"Where are we? Why did you bring us here?" Austin asked.

The sage stuck his hand out and waved it in front of everyone. "There is a great darkness that surrounds one of you. You are not welcome here."

"There is no darkness. I would have sensed it. We are only here to help," Yin said.

"Why have you returned?" the sage asked, pointing at Yin.

"Returned?" Yin asked.

Everyone looked at each other with a confused look on their faces.

"Ahh, you do not remember. The Great Yin. God of Light has forgotten," the sage said. "The last time you were here, you nearly destroyed the world. Allow me to remind you." The sage pointed at a chair in the temple. Yin walked over slowly. He turned back to look at Austin and the rest of the group as he sat down. The sage started chanting, mumbling something under his breath. It sounded like a hum. His staff started glowing. He held the staff up to Yin's head, and Yin's eyes began to glow. The sage turned to look

at the rest of the group "Long ago, when The Storm struck
down Yin, Yin's memory was broken. Only bits and pieces
survived. Others were lost. Yin fought off a God here in
Egypt."

"Wait, wasn't The Storm was the only other God to
come to Earth?" Olivia asked.

"There was another. An extremely dangerous God.
Yang's right hand. Destruction follows him everywhere.
Leaving behind nothing but fire and ash," the sage said.

Austin then realized something. "The museum!
The library of Alexandria was burnt to ash. All they found
was a raven feather. That God must have been the one to
destroy the library."

"Correct. Yin was able to stop him before he could
completely destroy the lighthouse. All of Egypt was on fire
that day. Yin saved the people of Egypt," the sage said.

Marcus was nervously looking around the room
and at everyone.

"Well, that's good, right? he saved everyone.
Earlier, you sounded like you didn't want him back," Mr.
Davidson said.

"Yin is the reason he came in the first place. Yin is
to blame for the destruction long ago, just like him," the
sage said.

"Does this God have a name?" Marcus asked with
hesitation and nervousness in his voice.

"He is a nameless God. Just like Yin and Yang.
Those were names given to them by people. The Egyptians
referred to this one as Ra. God of the sun." Austin and
Olivia both just looked at each other.
Yin's eyes went back to normal, and the staff stopped
glowing.

"I was able to heal some of his memory," the sage said. "The sooner you all get out of Egypt, the better."

"Please. I am sorry for everything I did. We are here to stop it. To put an end to The Storm and to Yang's plans," Yin said.

"Whatever happened to Ra?" Olivia asked.

"No one knows. Some say Yin destroyed Ra. Others say Ra is back in the God's temple with the other Gods. Few say he still roams the Earth in his human form, too weak to carry on. Waiting for Yang."

Marcus was acting unusually odd. He took a few steps back when they were talking about Ra. He turned and walked back to where the car was. Austin saw this and turned to follow him.

"Hey, you okay?" Austin asked.

Marcus was taking deep breaths. "Yeah, I'll be fine."

"What's going on? You can tell me anything," Austin said.

"It's turning into a lot. At first, it was the huntsmen chasing us. Then Elsie got taken, and now we are looking for a weapon that can kill a God. You need to fight The Storm. Every time something new came up, I was along for the ride hoping this would end soon. But now there's this Ra guy and Yang. What if they both come for us? What if other Gods come? I don't know if I can handle it," Marcus said.

Yin walked over "Don't worry. Whatever comes our way, Austin and I will handle it. We just need your help keeping everyone else safe."

"Yeah, when The Storm came during prom, you drove the car into one of his lions. You helped me. You kept me safe. I can't do this without you," Austin said.

Marcus rubbed his eyes and just shook his head. "Yeah, okay. Whatever I can do to help."

"And listen, if it gets to be too much, you can take a step back. That's fine," Austin said.

"What you seek is waiting," the sage said. Everyone turned around to look at the sage. He held his staff up high and slammed it on the ground. Once again, a cloud of sand surrounded everyone. When the sand faded, they were back on the road. The sage was gone. The car started up by itself. They all got back in the car and took off toward Alexandria.

"I wonder what other secrets we will discover since your memory was broken," Austin said, looking at Yin.

"I guess we will find out together," Yin responded.

The whole car ride was quiet. Austin, Olivia, and Marcus were asleep. Yin was staring out the window, and Mr. Davidson was reading a book on the history of Egypt. When Austin woke up, they had just pulled the city of Alexandria. Austin's dad parked the car, and everyone climbed out.

Mr. Davidson pulled out a map of Alexandria. "Okay, so here we are," pointing at the map. "The lighthouse is on the other side of the city. It's pretty crowded, so it's best we go on foot. That way, we can cut right through and not drive around."

As they were on their way to the lighthouse, they passed a few shops. One of which had some paintings. Austin was looking in at each shop as he passed. He stopped, turned around, and walked back to look back at a shop that he passed. He noticed a painting.

"Everything okay?" Olivia asked. Everyone stopped and turned around to see what Austin was doing. Olivia walked back to him.

"Look, that's just like the one in the museum," Austin was pointing at a painting. It looked very similar to the one with a man standing in fire with glowing white eyes. Austin walked in to talk to the shop owner. "Excuse me, sir," Austin said. The shop owner turned around. "Where did you get this painting? Do you know who painted it?"

The shop owner just stared at him.

"Did you hear me?" Austin asked.

"I'm so sorry to bother you," said a stranger in the shop. "He doesn't speak English very well. You see, the primary language here is Arabic. He might have understood two words from what you said. If you want, I could translate for you," offered the stranger.

"That would be amazing," Austin said. Olivia quickly grabbed his arm and pulled him away, "We need to think about this."

"Thank about what? We need to talk to him, and this guy can translate for us," Austin said.

"Don't you think it's a little weird that this guy can translate for us just as soon as we need a translator? What if he's a spy for The Storm?" Olivia asked.

"Good point. I won't give too much detail." Austin turned around and asked the stranger to translate for him. The stranger asked why they were interested in the painting.

"It's a personal interest," Austin said. Not wanting to give up too much detail. The stranger translated for Austin. The shop owner said he got the painting from the owner who was the oldest man in Alexandria. No one had seen him for years. Sometimes he showed up randomly for food and water, but no one knew where he lived or if he was still alive.

"Austin, Olivia! We need to go. We are losing daylight," Mr. Kale yelled into the shop. "We need to get to the lighthouse now."

"The lighthouse?" the stranger asked.

"It's for a school project," Olivia said quickly as she grabbed Austin's arm and ran out of the store.

"Maybe he was just a helpful, curious stranger," Austin said as they were walking to meet up with the group.

"We can't be too careful," Olivia replied, "we made it this far. We need to play it safe."

"Find anything out about the painting?" Marcus asked.

"Not really. Just that there's someone here they call the oldest man in Alexandria, and he was the man who painted it. But no one knows where he is or if he's even alive, so there goes that plan," Austin said.

"Let's just stick to the original," Olivia said.

They went past the rest of the shops and finally saw the water. They saw the church that was built after the original lighthouse fell.

"We are so close," Austin said as he stared out over the water to the church.

"Alexandria is the largest city on the Mediterranean. Also known as the Bride of the Mediterranean. The lighthouse was used to guide ships into this harbor, and it was the second largest construction after the pyramids. It was destroyed after a series of earthquakes between the years 1303 and 1323. People say it was the very first lighthouse. In the year 1477, the church was built around the surviving part of the lighthouse using the original stones," Mr. Davidson said.

"What would we do without that brain?" Marcus asked.

"Well, let's not waste any time," Austin said as he started to walk down the road leading to the Citadel of Qaitbay, an old fort that defended the city of Alexandria. When they got to the Citadel, they made their way through and found the exit. The exit was blocked off and security guards were walking around.

"Well, now how are we going to get through?" Olivia asked.

"I have a plan. Just wait for my signal," Yin said as he walked away.

"How will we know what the signal is?" Marcus asked Austin.

"I have no idea," Austin responded. A few seconds later, all the security guards ran away toward some commotion going on in the courtyard.

"I guess that's the signal," Austin's dad said. He opened the door, and everyone snuck out the back exit.

"What about Yin?" Olivia asked. They all looked up when they heard a raven's caw. The raven landed right next to them and transformed backed to Yin.

"So, what did you do back there?" Austin asked.

"I may have started a fire in the courtyard," Yin responded.

"Well, Good job," Mr. Kale said. "Come on. We better hurry before someone sees us out here."

They ran to the door of the church. It was empty, with no guards anywhere. When they walked in, they saw the top of the original lighthouse of Alexandria.

"Hello, beautiful," Mr. Davidson said. "This right here is one of the seven wonders of the ancient world. And I'm only a few steps away from it." Mr. Davidson couldn't take his eyes off it. He took a few pictures and took some notes for his history book. They began searching around the church for any clues or signs. About an hour went by, and still nothing.

"Maybe we missed it?" Olivia asked.

"No, we couldn't have," Austin said, looking around more.

"It's okay. We can find a different way to beat The Storm," Marcus said.

"No, I'm not giving up," Austin said. He turned around to look at the lighthouse. He noticed something on the lighthouse. He walked up to it and rubbed his hand over a symbol carved into the side of the lighthouse. It was a carving of a raven.

"The lighthouse is the clue," Austin said to himself. He looked into where the light would have come from and saw a small circular indent. He rubbed his fingers over the indent. Austin looked up and saw the light shining in from an opening in the roof. Everyone was watching him. "Wait!" he said. He reached into his pocket and pulled out the gold coin Yin gave him at the beginning of the school year. "Today is the longest day of the year. The sun will soon be at the highest point on the longest day." Austin said to the group. He placed the coin in the indent. As the sun slowly moved to the highest point in the sky, sunlight began to shine straight down onto the lighthouse. The light bounced off the coin and reflected in a wall of the church. "That's it?" Austin asked. "All that just to have the light point at a wall?" Austin sat down with his face in his hands. "We are never going to find it."

"Austin, look!" Olivia said, pointing at the wall. The light reflection was slowly moving on the wall. "The sun isn't at full height yet," Mr. Davidson said, pointing up at the sun.

"There's something else written here, I can't quite translate it though," Austin's dad said. Mr. Davidson came over to translate it with his book. "It looks like it's Arabic. It translates to *'through the looking glass'*."

"What's a looking glass?" Marcus asked.

"Well, Marcus, we call it a mirror," Mr. Davidson said. "You see, early mirrors, or looking glass, were created by Egyptians and the Greeks. They used polished bronze to create the looking glass."

"But there are no mirrors around, and what does it mean through the looking glass?" Marcus asked.

Austin was looking around the church. He saw a decent size mirror behind where the father of the church preaches.

"You aren't serious, are you?" Olivia asked.

"We'll put it back. We didn't come all this way for nothing," Austin said.

Mr. Kale, Marcus, and Mr. Davidson picked up the mirror and carried it over to the wall that the light was shining on. Slowly the light hit the mirror. Austin and Olivia looked in the mirror. Words in Arabic started to appear. Austin went and took Mr. Davidson's place and held the mirror so Mr. Davidson could see the words.

"Okay, so it looks like it says, *'the last light of the solstice'*," Mr. Davidson said, putting the book back in his pack.

"Sunset?" Olivia asked.

"That's what it sounds like to me," Austin's dad said.

"But what at sunset?" Marcus asked. "Will something happen?"

"I have no idea," Mr. Davidson said.

"So now what?" Austin asked.

"Wait..." Mr. Davidson said, going back to look at the writing on the lighthouse, "it says THROUGH the looking glass. What if it's showing us what we need to look at?"

Olivia tilted her head a little. The light that was reflecting off the coin was hitting the mirror. Olivia could see that it looked like the light was shining through the mirror and pointing at a cliffside out the window on the opposite side of the church. "It's pointing to a cliffside over there!" Olivia said, pointing out the window opposite them.

"But what if it doesn't lead anywhere? What if the lighthouse use to point in the right direction, but after it fell, it wasn't able to anymore? We would have wasted all this time when we could have been fighting The Storm." Marcus said.

"Only one way to find out," Austin said as he reached in and grabbed the coin from the lighthouse. "Let's go see that cliffside."

Chapter 14

A Trip Into History

Austin and the group made their way back through the Citadel without any problems. They were walking toward the cliff side that the lighthouse led them to. It looked over the Mediterranean Sea.

"Yin, can I ask you something?" Austin asked.

"Yes, of course," Yin responded. Austin and Yin were in the back of the group. They slowed down and let the others get farther ahead. Olivia looked back, but Austin waved her on. She nodded her head, turned, and kept walking.

"What's on your mind?" Yin asked.

"What if I can't beat him?" Austin asked.

"The Storm?"

Austin just nodded.

"Why would you even ask that?" Yin asked him.

"What if I'm not strong enough? I know we are looking for the sword, but what if we can't find it? The last time I tried hitting him, he didn't even flinch, and I ended up in the hospital." Austin said.

"I won't let that happen. I'll be with you the whole time," Yin said, trying to make Austin feel better about it.

"Yeah, but even you said that your power isn't what it used to be after stopping Yang from coming here," Austin said.

"Yes, that's true, but she isn't stopping me from protecting you."

"I barely know how to use my powers. How am I going to take on a powerful God?" Austin asked.

"Austin," Yin said. "You are more powerful than you think. If you fight with your heart, you won't lose. Plus, you have something he doesn't."

"Yeah, what's that?" Austin's asked.

"Something worth fighting for," Yin said as he smiled. "I'll tell you a secret. Every God is limited. Each one can only control a specific thing. The Storm is unique. He has the wind, rain, and lightning at his command. You, on the other hand, are different. You are the Son of Light." Yin put his arm around Austin. They turned and looked back at Alexandria. "Take a look. What do you see?" Yin asked.

"I see the ocean and Alexandria," Austin said.

"No, no, no," Yin said, shaking his head. "Look harder. What do you see?"

Austin took a deep breath. "I see the ocean crashing on the sand, trees blowing in the wind. Rocks on the ground. I see the light touching everything."

Yin turned to Austin, "Everything you see is at your command."

Yin turned to face the ocean. He held his hand out and closed his eyes. Making sure he kept his focus. Austin looked to the sea. The waters became calm. No waves, the whole sea was smooth. He held his other hand out toward the trees. Austin turned around to look. The wind stopped blowing. Not a single leaf was moving. Austin turned back toward Yin. Yin held both his hands out wide, palms facing up. Rocks of all sizes around them started floating. Yin slowly brought his hands closer to his body and then moved them straight out in front of him. The rocks began to move wherever Yin commanded.

"That was amazing, Yin," Austin said.

"There is one more thing. Every God has this ability when they become their most powerful," Yin said.

"You mean when your eyes light up?" Austin asked.

"Yes, that's it. It takes a long time for a God to master that. Unfortunately, Storm had already mastered it. Hurricane Katrina is an excellent example of his power," Yin said.

"Well, let's hope he doesn't do that when I face him," Austin said, "You think I'll ever be able to have the power?"

Yin was silent. Looking at Austin and then out toward the ocean.

"Yin?" Austin asked.

"Unfortunately, due to the fact, you are not fully God. You will not be able to use this power. Your human half is blocking you," Yin said to Austin.

"Oh, okay," Austin said, trying to hide the disappointment. "Well, hopefully, I won't ever have to use that power. I mean, we will have the sword, right?" Austin asked, trying to stay positive.

"That's right," Yin said with a smile. They walked to catch up with the group.

"Don't worry. We will practice your powers," Yin said.

The group arrived at the cliffside. It was about a mile away from the lighthouse. They all put their packs down. Mr. Davidson was prepared. He packed a propane tank and a mini grill to make sandwiches for everyone. While they were eating, Yin and Austin were a few yards away practicing. Austin tried over and over again to move a rock, but he just couldn't. "I don't understand. At prom, I made a wall of light energy and now nothing?" Austin asked.

"At the moment, you acted before thinking. Sometimes that works out. You were faced with danger, and it just happened. Now you're just doing it to do it. Focus. You control it. The rock is at your command."

Austin took a deep breath. He was focusing hard on a rock in front of him. He stood just like Yin was before. Austin held his hands out wide, palms facing up, staying focused. Austin saw the rock move a little.

"Did you see that?!" Austin asked in excitement, pointing at the rock.

"I did. That's a start," Yin replied.
He kept practicing for the next hour or so. He ran over to the group. "Guys, look what I can do." Austin closed his eyes and held his hand out. Using all his focus, a rock flew up into his palm.

"So, you're a Jedi?" Marcus asked. Everyone laughed.

"That was really amazing," Olivia said.

"I still need a lot more practice if I'm going to face The Storm, though," Austin said.

"You'll do great," Olivia reassured him.

Once everyone was done eating and well rested and refreshed with water, they agreed they should start looking for a clue. They had about four hours until sunset. That meant only four hours to find a clue.

One hour went by, and no clue was found. They seemed to have skimmed over the cliffside very quickly. They agreed to slow down and look harder.

One more hour went by. Still have no clue. This time they decided to widen the range of where they were looking.

One more hour went by, meaning one more hour left. Still, no clue had been found. They had been trying everything. They climbed up higher to see if they could find one from a different angle. They stood far back to see if it was something big they were missing. Still no luck. They had one hour left. Every ten minutes, they turned around and saw the sun setting. They were running around trying to find anything that could help them. The moon was in the sky with only twenty minutes left until the sunlight was gone. They had twenty minutes to find an unknown clue. Austin was getting more frustrated with each passing minute.

"Maybe the lighthouse wasn't working properly. I mean, it is over two thousand years old," Olivia said.

Austin fell to his knees with his hands on his head. "This can't be how it ends. All this time wasted. How are we going to get Elsie back now?"

Austin's dad knelt down next to him, "Don't worry. We will find another way. We won't stop until we get her back."

Austin lifted his head up. He watched as the last light of the sun disappeared. All hope was lost. Everyone just hung their heads, upset and disappointed that they were not able to find why the lighthouse pointed to the cliff side.

"Now what are we going to do?" Austin asked, trying to hold back the tears.

"We just keep on going. We will stop at nothing until Elsie is safe and The Storm is gone." Austin's dad said.

"I'm in," Olivia said.

"Me too," Marcus added.

"I'm not going anywhere," Mr. Davidson said. Austin looked at Yin. Yin smiled and nodded.

"Okay," Austin said as he stood up, rubbing his eyes. Everyone was walking back to Alexandria. Austin was walking the slowest. He looked down as he was walking. He reached into his pocket and pulled out the gold coin Yin gave him. Austin stopped walking as he saw the eye of the raven on the coin was glowing. He quickly looked up at the moon, then back at the cliffside. There was something glowing.

"Hey! Wait!" Austin yelled. Everyone turned around. "The last light of the solstice wasn't sunset. It's the light of the moon," he added as he was pointing up at the moon. "The moonlight is the last light of the day," he pointed back at the cliffside, and they all saw something glowing. They all ran back to see what it was. Once they got there, they saw a small glowing indent that they didn't see in the daylight. Austin held the coin up to the glow, and a rock wall on the cliffside collapsed, revealing a cave.

"Okay, now that was cool," Marcus said.
The group ran over to the cave entrance.

"Does Anyone want to go first into the dark cave?" Marcus asked.

Austin took a few steps into the cave. "Come on." Everyone started walking into the cave. Mr. Davidson noticed a torch hanging on the cave wall. He grabbed a lighter from his bag, grabbed the torch off the wall and lit it. Now they had light to see. As they walked deeper into the cave and around corners, they came to a five-way split. They heard a crunch on the ground as they were walking. Olivia looked down and saw she had stepped on a human skull. She started screaming. There were human remains all on the ground.

"I guess other people tried getting here before us," Mr. Kale said.

"Well, let's not end up like them," Mr. Davidson said.

Austin turned and looked back at the tunnels. There were little cave paintings all over the walls and above the tunnels.

"How do we pick which way to go?" Marcus asked.

"Austin, look," Olivia said, pointing at a painting of a raven. The only raven painting in the cave.

"The raven led us this far," Austin said, looking at Yin. The raven painting was over the tunnel second to the right. After a long winding tunnel, it eventually opened to a big dark room. There was a stone block in front of them with a bowl on top and liquid inside.

Mr. Davidson walked up and dipped his finger in the bowl, and then smelled his fingers. "It's oil." He took the torch and put the flame on the oil. The fire began traveling along a stone wall with oil on top, lighting up the big room. It was full of scrolls and old books, and ancient-looking artifacts. Mr. Davidson fell to his knees. "Oh my God," he

A God Among Men

said as he put his hand over his mouth. "This is..." he began.

"The Library of Alexandria," a voice said from the dark. A very old man walked into the light. "I wondered when you would be returning, God of Light."
Everyone looked at Yin.

"Who are you?" Austin asked.

"My name is Ammon," he said.

"You know me?" Yin asked.

"Yes, of course. I would not be here if it weren't for you," he said.

"What are you doing down here?" Marcus asked.

"Protecting the library just like you did many years ago," Ammon said, looking at Yin. "I have been down here for as long as I can remember."

"Are you the one they call the oldest man in Alexandria?" Austin asked.

"Let's see, a few months ago was my one thousand nine hundred and eleventh birthday. How long are people living nowadays?" Ammon asked with a smile. Everyone's eyes widened as their jaws dropped. Everyone, other than Yins.

"So, you must have made the painting with Yin" Olivia said.

"Painting? - ah yes, now I remember. I did that painting the night of the great fire. I remember it like it was yesterday. The God of The Sun, Ra, was burning the city of Alexandria, orders from Yang. He was about to burn the library until you stopped Ra," Ammon was pointing at Yin. "You shook the Earth and buried the library in order to protect it. The fire destroyed everything in its path. You made it look like the fire successfully destroyed it. You

- 172 -

tricked the Gods. All that was left after the fire was a single raven feather, which I believe now sits in the museum."

"Why would he save the library?" Marcus asked.

"The library, young man, holds the world's most illustrious collections of scrolls and books. Even some about the Gods themselves," Ammon said.

"So, Yang must have wanted to destroy the library so no one would know anything about them," Austin's dad said.

"We are looking for something. A sword shaped like a raven's feather. Have you seen anything like that or read anything about it?" Austin asked.

"Oh no. No weapons down here. And I have not read a single thing down here. I am not worthy of this knowledge. I am only here to protect it. You are more than welcome to look around," Ammon said. He turned and walked back to another room in the library.

"Well, we made it this far. Let's not stop now. Everyone take a section, and let's see what we can find," Mr. Kale said.

The group split up and started looking. Trying to read old books was not the easiest. The pages were so frail they had to be extra careful. Scrolls were wrapped around a bronze tube with a flat part at the end with a symbol on it to mark what it was about.

"This must have been how they sorted scrolls in history. A historic Dewey decimal system. Amazing!" Mr. Davidson said.

"What do you think this is?" Olivia asked, holding up a chain with an upside-down pyramid hanging from it. There was an Egyptian eye on the front of the pyramid.

"I'm not sure, but we need to be extra careful with everything in here," Austin said.

Olivia carefully places the artifact down next to one that looked like a necklace, rod and a few others. She started looking at scrolls. One had an image of the same artifact she picked up.

"Who in the world is David, and why did he take a slingshot to a sword fight against a giant?" Mr. Kale said after reading a scroll.

"Did you guys know the world was covered in water for over a month? These scrolls are crazy," Austin said.

"Hey Austin, come look at this," Marcus said. Austin went over to where Marcus was looking. There was a bronze piece in a pile of ash. The image on the bronze piece was a picture of the sun. "I guess Ra was able to destroy something about him after all," Marcus said, looking at the pile of ash on the ground.

"That doesn't change anything. Let's keep looking," Austin said.

"Hey, I think I found something!" Olivia yelled. She was in the second to last aisle of scrolls. Everyone ran over to her. "I've looked all over, and this is the only one with a picture of a raven on it." Olivia grabbed the scroll and slowly picked it up, making sure not to damage anything. She slowly unrolled the scroll. There was only one line written on the scroll.

Three kings will help you find, that of which was lost in time.

"Lost in time?" Mr. Kale asked.

"Three kings?" Olivia also asked.

Austin was thinking hard. "The pyramids?" He asked.

Everyone turned to him.

"Pyramids?" Marcus asked as he was confused.

"No, don't say it like that. Hear me out. What if the pyramids, one of the most ancient structures in the world, are protecting the sword?" Austin asked.

"Austin, this doesn't really say 'go to the pyramids' to me," Olivia said, holding up the scroll.

"Just think about it. The pyramids were built after three kings of Egypt," Austin said.

"It's not as crazy as we think," Mr. Davidson said. "The pyramids were originally built as shrines to the Gods. After the humans rebelled, they were turned into tombs for the kings of Egypt. Humans worshiped the kings or Pharaohs more than the Gods, so they were given the pyramids as their final resting place. It does sound like a good spot to put a God-killing weapon."

"Don't you think they would have looked there?" Marcus asked.

"Maybe they didn't know where to look," Mr. Kale said. "It's worth a shot."

They all agreed and decided to leave the library of Alexandria. They thanked Ammon, and he welcomed them back anytime. He told them that they can only find the entrance once a year. The knowledge in this place is too great for any man to have. They decided not to talk about it and to keep its location a secret. They walked back through the tunnel and back out to the cliffside. Once they were all outside, Yin turned around and held his hand up. Rocks crumbled and buried the cave entrance.

A God Among Men

"The library will remain protected," Yin said.

The group turned and put the library behind them, never to speak of it again. Each one held some knowledge of what they read and saw down there. For now, they were headed off to the pyramids.

Meanwhile, in Norway, The Storm had his men preparing his ship. They carried a cage onto the ship with Elsie inside. "Make sure she's fed," he demanded. "But, sir, we only have enough food for the crew," one of his men said.

"Are you part of the crew?" Storm asked. The man just nodded his head. The Storm struck him down instantly. He turned to more of his men. "Do we have enough now!?" He yelled.

His men just nodded their heads and ran on board in fear. He walked onto the ship. The cage Elsie was in was right next to his seat in his chambers. Once they set sail, Elsie asked where they were going.

"I think it's about time I rid the world of your brother and his crusade. Once I'm finished with him and Yin, the world will finally have its Queen, Yang. And I'll be right there by her side," The Storm said.

There was some commotion on the ship, and a red and orange flash shone through the window of his quarters. As soon as he stood up, the door flung open.

"Who dares disturb..." before The Storm could finish, a hooded man entered the room. A red fog traveled along the ground. It didn't look like the man was even walking. Not a bounce in his step. He just glided across the ground. Elsie tried to see who it was, but all she saw were glowing red eyes. His face was covered in shadows.

"What a surprise. I thought you were dead. What brings you here... Ra?" The Storm asked.

Elsie was hoping to hear his voice, but all she could hear was an echoey hiss. She couldn't make out a single word.

"He's in Egypt? I'll make him come to me. I have something he wants," The Storm said as he looked at Elsie. Ra didn't turn his head at all.

"Don't worry. I'll do what you couldn't," The Storm said to Ra.

Elsie heard the hissing again. She even closed her eyes to try and focus on the noise to make out words, but still nothing.

Something must have angered The Storm. "How dare you threaten me!" he yelled. "You are weak. You lost your power the moment you lost the eternal flame!"

Ra looked right up at The Storm. He started to float in the air and a bright red light shinned in from the windows. He held his hands up, but the arms of the cloak were covering his hands, so Elsie couldn't see anything. The wind started slamming the door and windows open and closed over and over again. A harsh hiss filled the air, and The Storm sat back in his seat in fear of Ra. The light faded, the wind stopped, and Ra was back on the ground. He glided backward and out the door. The red fog left with him. The Storm was extremely angry. Elsie had never seen him this angry. One of his men knocked on the door, and instantly The Storm threw lightning at the door. The door and the man both burst into smoke.

"Austin Kale's head will hang on my wall. That will show Yang I'm her right hand over Ra!" Storm yelled clenching his fist.

A God Among Men

Elsie looked up and could see out the window. There was an extremely dark storm cloud forming in the sky. Elsie was scared before, but this was a whole new level of fear she had never felt before.

Chapter 15
The Three Kings

After leaving the Library of Alexandria, the group decided to go back to the hotel and sleep. It had been an eventful day, and they were exhausted. In the middle of the night, Austin heard a noise and looked over and saw Marcus wasn't in his bed. He heard the noise again. A creaking noise. He slowly and quietly moved to the front door. He opened it and poked his head out. He looked up and down the hallway but did not see anything. He heard the noise again. This time it was coming from the bathroom. He turned around and slowly put his hand on the doorknob. He flung the door open. Marcus was bent over throwing up in the toilet.

"Jeez, you scared me," Austin said.

"I scared you? You scared me. What are you doing bursting in here like that?" Marcus asked.

"I heard a noise. I didn't know what it was," Austin said.

"It was me. I tried being quiet. I opened the window to get some fresh air in here. It must have been something I ate," Marcus said as he grabbed his stomach and leaned back over the toilet.

"I hope you feel better, man," Austin said as he patted him on the back and then went back to bed.

Eventually, Marcus got himself back in bed, and they both slept until morning. The sun shined bright through the hotel window. Austin woke up, got out of bed, put some clothes on, and went out on the balcony. He stared at the pyramids. Marcus eventually came out and sat there with him.

"You think it could really be in there?" Marcus asked.

"I have no idea. For hundreds of years, explorers have searched the pyramids. If they couldn't find it, how are we going to?" Austin replied.

"We've been lucky thus far. Hopefully, we have some luck left," Marcus added. There was a knock on their door. It was the rest of the group.

"You ready?" Austin's dad asked.

"As I'll ever be," Austin said. Marcus patted him on the back. "We got this," he said. They headed down the hallway to the stairs and through the lobby. They got in the car and drove toward the Great Pyramids.

Olivia was looking at her phone. "Austin, look," she showed him the weather app, and there was a very large storm forming. One of the largest they had ever seen.

"Is that-?" Olivia asked.

"The Storm," Austin finished. "He must be on the move. We don't have any time to waste."

"So, what's the plan? Just walk right into the pyramids? Which one are we picking first?" Marcus asked.

"It's not going to be that easy. There are things guarding the pyramids. And I'm going to guess the Great

Pyramid." Mr. Davidson said. They parked the car, and all got out.

"What do you mean, things?" Marcus asked.

Mr. Davidson pointed up behind Marcus. Marcus turned around and saw the Great Sphinx.
"The sphinx is the guardian of the pyramids," Mr. Davidson said.

"Well, I think it'll be easy getting past him," Marcus said. Everyone laughed.

"There are guards that patrol the pyramids. The largest one is the most protected," Mr. Davidson said.

"Okay, so how do we get inside?" Olivia asked.

"There are two entrances to the pyramid. There is a main entrance at the base of the pyramid, but there is a much less guarded entrance on the opposite side, up toward the middle of the pyramid," Mr. Davidson said.

"Okay, so the less guarded one it is," Mr. Kale said.

There were ropes around the pyramid. Yin walked over to the guards standing on that side while everyone else snuck under the rope and began climbing up to the entrance. Yin was distracting the guards by just asking them questions and asking for directions. Once Yin saw everyone was up near the entrance, he thanked the guards for their help and walked away to where the guards couldn't see. The guards turned around to make sure nothing fishy was going on, but they didn't see anything. Everyone was lying down flat. The angle at which the guards were looking made it easy for the group to hide. Yin flew and landed right next to them as a raven. When the guards turned back around, he flapped his wings, and everyone got up quietly and went inside the pyramid. Once they were inside, they closed the entrance.

"We made it in. Let's go," Marcus said as he took a step. When his foot landed on the ground, everyone heard a click. Marcus looked down. He had stepped on a trap. The floor below them fell, and they all slid down into the pyramid.

"Did I mention the Egyptians designed traps in the pyramids to protect the Pharos from grave robbers? We all need to be careful," Mr. Davidson said as he and everyone got up. He pulled out his lighter and lit it, so they had some light. They had fallen into a large room inside the pyramid. There was a doorway on the other side of the room. A small pathway with pits on each side. Spikes lay at the bottom of those pits, along with the skeletons of those who tried and failed.

"Why am I worried about just walking to the other side of the room?" Austin asked.

"Because it looks too easy," Marcus said. He started walking along the path.

"Marcus, no! stop!" Austin's dad yelled. Marcus turned around and heard a click from a wall. He jumped back, and an arrow landed right where he stood.

"What was that?! The pyramid tried to kill me!" Marcus yelled.

"We need to be careful," Austin said.

Mr. Davidson was looking at a statue in the room. He turned around and saw another one. They were standing the same way. With their left foot forward. He decided to try and walk the skinny path.

"Mr. Davidson, what are you doing?" Olivia asked.

"Trust me," he said back. He walked along the path keeping his left foot forward. He didn't realize this at first, but every time he moved his left foot, it landed on a small pressure-plated stone, keeping the arrows from being shot out.

"You see, we are in the pharaoh's tomb. We need to show our respect to the Pharaoh. In ancient Egypt, when someone would approach the king of Egypt, they would put their left foot forward."

"Why your left foot?" Marcus asked.

"Good question, and here's why. Your heart is on your left side. When you put your left foot forward, you are putting your heart forward toward the Pharaoh. It's a sign of respect. Because if you did not respect him, you ended up dead. Just like you would here," Mr. Davidson said.

"That's amazing that you figured that out, Mr. Davidson," Olivia said.

"I am living my dream right now. The lighthouse, standing inside the library of Alexandria and now exploring the Great Pyramid. Thank you, Austin, for letting me come along for this journey," Mr. Davidson said to Austin.

Austin smiled. "Of course. We wouldn't have made it this far without you."

They all began walking along the path with their left foot forward. Mr. Davidson turned to look in the next doorway. Austin's dad was helping everyone come across as he was the second to cross after Mr. Davidson. Marcus was the last to walk along the path. They heard a click.

"Marcus!" Olivia yelled.

"It wasn't me! My left foot is forward!" Marcus yelled back. "Did I do something wrong?!"

No one saw any arrows shoot out.

"What was that noise?" Austin asked, "Mr. Davidson do you know what that was? Did we do something wrong?"

A God Among Men

Mr. Davidson was standing in the doorway. He didn't say anything.

"Mr. Davidson?" Olivia asked.

Mr. Davidson started to turn around. Taking small, sloppy steps. He looked up at everyone. His shirt was turning bloody, with an arrow sticking out of his chest.

"No!" Austin yelled. He ran over to Mr. Davidson as he collapsed to the ground.

Everyone else followed. Marcus was still on the path but ran and put his right foot forward. There was another click, and an arrow shot out. Marcus screamed and fell to the ground. Olivia turned around to see Marcus on the ground holding his leg. There was an arrow sticking out of his right leg. She ran over to try and help him. It went all the way through his leg. Mr. Kale ran over to help Marcus. He snapped the sharp part of the arrow off and pulled the other half out the opposite way. He took his belt off and wrapped it around Marcus's leg. He also ripped a piece of his shirt off and wrapped it around the wound.

Once Marcus was taken care of as much as they could, they turned to look at Austin and Mr. Davidson. He was lying in Austin's arms. He started coughing up blood.

Austin looked up at Yin. "Do something. Help him!" Austin yelled as tears rolled down his face. "Anyone?" He asked, looking at his dad, Olivia, and Marcus. Each one started to have tears roll down as well. Yin knelt next to Austin. "I'm sorry. Not even I can put a stop to death."

"Dad, do you have a first aid kit?" Austin yelled through his tears. Austin's dad just closed his eyes and hung his head. Olivia turned and cried into Mr. Kale's chest. Marcus was lying on the ground and just hung his head as tears fell.

Yin put his arm around Austin. "He's gone." Austin looked up at Yin and back to Mr. Davidson. Not coughing, not breathing. Yin put his hand over Mr. Davidson's eyes to close them. Austin, in shock, couldn't believe what just happened. The room was silent. For the next half hour, they all sat there. Austin didn't move at all.

Austin's dad got up to check on Marcus. "How's your leg?" he asked.

"I can still feel my toes. I'm not sure how much pressure I could put on it," Marcus said.

Austin laid Mr. Davidson down on the ground. "He looked at Yin. Can you guide everyone back outside? Make sure they get home. And take his body back home also." Austin said, looking down at Mr. Davidson.

"And what are you going to do?" Olivia asked.

"I'm finishing this alone," Austin said.

"Like hell you are." she said back. Olivia was angry at the thought of Austin trying to do this by himself. "We all agreed to come to help you. I'm not leaving."

"No, you don't get it! It's real now! This isn't some walk in the park, here's the treasure, now you win. You can get hurt. I'm not going to let anyone else die trying to help me," Austin said with anger in his voice.

"Now it's real?!" Olivia fired back. "It has been real for all of us! You were in the hospital for weeks! We didn't know if you would be the same or make it through that. I can't leave knowing you are risking your life. Either we come with you, or you leave with us."

Austin looked around at everyone. He nodded his head, "Okay. We do this together."

"I'll get Mr. Davidson out. Just be careful," Yin said.

A God Among Men

Austin turned to the doorway and laid down on the ground. He saw that one of the stones was slightly raised. That must have been the pressure-plated stone. They needed to be careful. There could be more.

"I'm going to wait here. I'll just slow you down," Marcus said. "Just promise you'll come back for me."

"I'll come to get you after I get Mr. Davidson out," Yin said.

Olivia, Austin, and his dad proceeded into the next room. From where they were standing, it looked much larger than the previous room. There were walls all around them, but open space above the walls. The walls were about 8 feet tall. Austin and his dad decided to lift Olivia up to have her look over the top. She saw walls all over the place and a door on the far side of the room.

"We might be in trouble," she said as they let her back down.

"Why is that?" Mr. Kale asked.

"I think this is a maze, and judging by the last room, it might have traps around each corner," Olivia said.

"What do we do now?" Austin's dad said. "How are we going to get through this?"

Austin closed his eyes. He could hear Yin's voice in his head, "You are more powerful than you think. Everything is at your command" he remembered when Yin first took him and showed him the small town that was destroyed by The Storm. Yin had him close his eyes and use his ears to hear everything. Austin, with his eyes closed, started to walk through the maze.

"Austin, get back here," his dad said.

"What are you doing?" Olivia asked.

Austin didn't respond. He took a step. He heard a stone under his foot move slightly. Then he heard a latch open and a click. An arrow shot out.

"Austin!" Olivia yelled.

Austin could hear the arrow cutting through the air. He rotated his body, and the arrow passed right by him. Olivia and Mr. Kale just looked at each other. Austin turned each corner, dodging arrow after arrow. He even caught a few in the air. Eventually, Austin got to the end of the maze without even opening his eyes. Olivia and Mr. Kale waited at the beginning. Mr. Kale had lifted Olivia up so she could keep an eye on him.

"You okay?" she yelled.

Austin opened his eyes. There were a few steps in front of him. He walked up and turned around to face the maze and saw Olivia looking over the top. "I'm okay!" Austin yelled back.

"We're going to stay here. We can't do what you just did. Just be careful!" she yelled back.

Austin turned around and walked through the doorway. He was keeping an eye out for traps but did not see any. Just a large gold box in the middle of a room. He slowly walked to the box, looking around the room. He didn't see any skeletons. He must have been the first person to reach that room. This was it, after all these clues, he had finally made it. He reached and opened the gold box, ready to find Aggon's sword and put an end to The Storm. He pushed the top of the box open... only to find it empty.

"No, no, no," he said over and over again. "It has to be here. Where's the sword?" He searched all around the room. It was completely empty other than the box.

He could hear Olivia yelling to him, "Everything okay?" Austin couldn't believe it. He turned and walked out of the room. This time he was able to walk on top of the maze. He reached his dad and Olivia.

"Well?" Olivia asked.

"The sword wasn't there," Austin said, disappointed.

"We were wrong?" Austin's dad asked.

"Unless someone beat us here," Austin said.

"Maybe Yang or The Storm found it before us," Olivia said.

"No, the lighthouse led us to the library, and the library led us here. We can't really go back to the library. The entrance is sealed again," Austin said.

"We can figure it out. For now, let's get out of here. Marcus is hurt," Mr. Kale said.

"Right, let's go," Austin said. They got to the room with the skinny path and walked backward on it, keeping their left leg forward. Austin just looked at the blood stain on the ground where Mr. Davidson laid.

"I won't let you down," he said.

They climbed back out of the pyramid. They must have been in there all day. The sun had set, and the moon and the stars were out. Yin saw them coming out and distracted the guards again. They were able to climb down the pyramid, and all met up back at the car.

Mr. Kale ran to check on Marcus's leg. "Well, did you find it?" Marcus asked them.

"There wasn't anything inside," Austin said.

"You'll need stitches. A doctor will have to take a look, but you should be fine," Mr. Kale said to Marcus.

"Nothing?" Marcus asked, "Now what?"

"I don't know," Austin said. "The library won't be available until next summer, and we can't exactly wait that long."

"What did the scroll say again?" Austin's dad asked.

"*Three kings will help you find, that of which was lost in time*," Austin said

Olivia had her hands on her head, trying to think. She was looking up at the sky. Her eyes widened, and her hands slowly dropped.

"Guys," she said. Everyone looked. She turned to look at them. "We didn't fail. We can still find the sword."

"What are you talking about?" Marcus asked.

"Look," Olivia turned to the sky and pointed up. "You see those three stars there? That's Orion's Belt, also known as the three kings. The Three Kings of Egypt built the pyramids to match those stars. Three kings will lead the way. The stars are pointing toward the mountains of Petra. There has been a big arrow right in front of us the whole time."

"It all sounds like a wild goose chase," Marcus said, "Why take us to the library and then all the way to Petra?"

"I think Olivia is right, think about it. First the sun helped with the lighthouse. Then the moon helped us find the library. Now I think it's time for the stars to help us," Austin said.

"Why couldn't there just be a map with an X on it that says 'here's the sword, have fun'?" Marcus asked.

"Because we're not pirates," Mr. Kale whispered to him as he laughed a little bit. "I'll meet you guys there. I'm going to arrange to have Mr. Davidson's body taken back home," Mr. Kale said to the group.

"We'll wait for you," Olivia said.

"Then what?" Marcus asked.

"Well, we got nothing else to lose. The mountains of Petra it is," Austin said as he looked off into the distance.

Chapter 16
The Lost City

The group went back to the hotel. Austin's dad was talking to Austin's mom on the phone.

"How is everything? Is everyone okay?" Austin's mom asked.

There was a pause.

"Brian?" she asked.

"There was an accident," Mr. Kale said.

"Austin?" she asked quickly.

"No, no, he's fine. It was Mr. Davidson."

"Oh my goodness, is he okay?" She asked.

"He umm…" there was another pause. "He didn't make it." Mr. Kale told Mrs. Kale about everything that happened since they landed. He asked if she would be able to claim the body when it landed back home. She said she would call a funeral home to pick up the body. Mr. Kale made sure to tell Mrs. Kale he loved her and Ava, and that they would be home as soon as they could.

After talking on the phone, Mr. Kale made arrangements at the airport to make sure Mr. Davidson made it home. They were still in shock about Mr. Davidson, so they stayed at the hotel overnight again. It was not an early morning like usual. Everyone seemed to have a hard time getting up without Mr. Davidson.

"We're going to a place we know nothing about," Austin said as he was lying in his bed, looking up at the ceiling.

"Mr. Davidson would know everything about the Petra Mountains," Marcus said as he also laid on his bed looking at the ceiling. "How do we even know where to look?"

"I'm sure we will know when we see it," Austin said.

There was a knock on the door. Austin got up to see who it was. Olivia and Mr. Kale were at the door. "Are you guys ready to go?" Mr. Kale asked, "We have a long car ride ahead of us."
Austin and Marcus grabbed their bags. They all got down to the lobby and out to the car. Yin was waiting for them. Two hours into the car ride, still no one said a word. Just a cough and a sneeze or two. Olivia and Marcus fell asleep. Austin stayed awake, looking back at the pyramids.

Another hour went by, and Marcus woke up. He stretched and yawned. "So," finally breaking the silence, "what do you think we're going to find when we get to Petra?" Marcus asked.

"Hopefully, what we've been looking for," Austin's dad said.

A few more hours went by. Austin's dad finally parked the car. He got out and opened the side door, and woke Austin, Olivia, and Marcus up. "Wake up. We're here," Mr. Kale said. Each one woke up and stretched. They climbed out of the car, grabbed their bags and continued on foot.

"I don't even know where to start," Marcus said.

"You'll know it when you see it," Austin said.

Each one looked all around random places of the mountain range as they were walking. Austin noticed a man in a cloak. "Hey!" he yelled.

"What is it?" Olivia asked as she ran over to him. Austin looked back to Olivia and back to where the man was standing. Only now, he was gone.

"Remember on the tour of the pyramids my dad set up for us? Do you remember that man I saw who was following us?" Austin asked.

"No, you were the only one who saw him. Do you remember that?" Olivia pulled a water bottle out of her bag and gave it to Austin. "Here, take a drink. Maybe it's the heat getting to you."

"I'm not seeing things," Austin said, turning away from Olivia.

She quickly grabbed his hand and made him turn back. She put her hand on his cheek. "Please drink some water. For me."

Austin agreed and took the water bottle.

"Better?" Olivia asked.

"Better," Austin said.

About an hour went by, and they still hadn't found anything.

"We should spread out more," Austin suggested. The group did just that, even though it didn't last long.

"Uhh, guys!" Olivia yelled. "I think I found it!" Everyone ran over to her.

"Out of this whole mountain range, what makes you think you found…. Woah," Marcus said as he ran over to where Olivia was standing. They were looking at the biggest doorway they had ever seen. Pillars, statues, and a doorway, all carved into the mountainside. They had never seen anything like this before.

They just stood with their mouths open.

"Mr. Davidson would have loved to see this," Austin said.

He took a few steps forward.

"Where are you going?" Marcus asked.

"We're not going to find what we are looking for out here," Austin said as he turned to walk into the doorway.

Everyone followed. There were carvings all inside but still no sword.

"What if the sword doesn't exist?" Marcus asked.

"It does," Yin said.

"How do you know?" Marcus asked.

"Because I was the one who made it," Yin said, looking at him.

"Oh, right," Marcus said as he went back to looking.

Austin was rubbing his hand along the wall with the carvings. He was a little way down from everyone else. There was a big carving of a raven. Austin was just staring at it. He could feel something calling out to him.

Olivia saw Austin standing there, so she walked over to him. She turned to look at the raven. She noticed one of the raven's eyes was missing. "Austin look," she said, pointing to the raven's left eye.

Austin reached into his pocket and pulled out the gold coin and placed it where the eye would be. The wall started the shake, and just to the right of them, a pathway opened. Everyone ran over to see what happened.

"Come on, it's this way," Austin said.

"How do you know?" Olivia asked.

"I just have a feeling," Austin said. He could feel something calling to him. They each walked into the dark tunnel. Once they were all inside the tunnel shut behind them.

"No turning back now," Austin's dad said.

There was a light at the end of the tunnel they could see. Once they reached it, their jaws dropped again. They were looking down at an entire underground city. Buildings made out of stone. Some were hanging from the ceiling of the giant cave they were in. Bridges made out of stone were connecting the buildings. Roads carved on the ground. Even an underground waterfall to a lake with a river running through the heart of this city.

They started hearing footsteps. Austin looked to his right and saw a group of men running toward them with spears. "Woah, Woah, Woah," Austin said as he put his hands up. Yin quickly grabbed his arms and forced Austin's hands down.

"What are you doing?" Austin asked.

"How would you feel if strangers just entered your home?" Yin asked Austin.

Austin realized Yin was right and stood down. One of the men held his spear close to Austin's neck. Austin was trying not to move at all.

"Who are you? What are you doing in our home?" one of the guards asked.

"Hello, the people call me Yin," Yin said, getting the attention off Austin. "You might know me as the God of Light."

A God Among Men

The guards looked at each other and put the spears down. The guards escorted Austin and the group down a path from where they entered. They were led through the city. The people of the city stared at them as they walked the streets. The windows were just holes cut out in the stone buildings. They could see people looking down at them. People on the streets were following them, creating a crowd. The guards took them to a stone pavilion. Men and women were sitting around a stone table.

One man, who sat in the biggest chair, stood up. "Who are you, and what are you doing here?"

"H-hello, sir," Austin said as he took a step forward. As soon as he moved, three guards held their spears up to his throat. "Okay, okay. I won't take any steps," Austin took a step back. He was looking all around him. "Uhh... my name is Austin." He kept looking at the guards and their spears. They were making him nervous. "These are my friends. We have come a long way."

"How did you find us?" the man asked.

"Well, we're here to find a sword. I'm not sure if you all know, but there is a very bad man up on the surface who is trying to take over the world. And that sword can help us defeat..." Austin couldn't finish.

"How did you find us?" the man asked again, only this time louder, as spears got closer.

"Well, clues lead us to a lighthouse which then pointed to an ancient library, which led us here. Then I used a special coin to open the door which led us to you." Austin said, looking at the point of a spear.

"Is it just the five of you?" the man asked.

"Yes, well, there was a sixth. But he's not here anymore," Austin said, lowering his head.

"Where is the sixth?" the man asked.

Austin took a short pause, "he... died."

"Do you have the coin?" he asked.

"Well, no. It's up in the..." Austin was interrupted.

"Do you have anything from the library?"

"No, we didn't want to take..." Austin was interrupted again.

"How did your friend die?"

"Well, we were actually in a pyramid and..." Austin was interrupted for the third time.

"No coin, no proof of library, now adding a pyramid to your story. You are lying. You must be the bad man you were talking about. Your fate is...execution!"

Austin just looked at the group. They were all scared and looking around. The men with spears started walking closer.

"One by one, you will each be executed for trespassing, lying, and attempted theft." the man said.

"Wait, we didn't steal anything!" Austin yelled.

"We're about to get executed, and he's worrying about us not stealing anything?" Marcus whispered to Olivia.

"Shut up," Olivia nudged Marcus.

"They will not!" a voice said, coming from a small stone hut. Everyone turned to look at the hut. Two men walked out. One was very old, a little hunched over, walking with a walking stick. The other was the person wearing the cloak that had been following them.

Everyone around them bowed down. Olivia looked next to her and saw Marcus bowing down.

"What? They are all doing it?" he said as he looked up at her.

She picked him up, "We don't bow to anyone."

The man from the chair was bowing down. He lifted his head as the old man got closer. "Sir, these people are..."

"Our guests," the old man interrupted.

"Yes, of course," the man said. He waved the guards to stand down. Austin and the group were more relaxed now without having spears at their faces and backs.

The old man got closer to Austin. "I've been expecting you, Austin Kale." The old man turned, "Walk with me."

Austin looked back at the group and then looked up at the man from the chair.

"Ignore him. Haru won't hurt you."

"Haru?" Austin asked, "His name is Haru. Got it." Austin said as he started walking toward the old man.

"You can tell the God of Light to join us," he said.

Austin was surprised he knew who they were. He turned to wave to Yin, telling him to join them. Yin, Austin, the old man, and the cloaked man began walking along the river.

"I was wondering when you would make it here," the old man said.

Austin kept looking over at the cloaked man. "Sir, if you were expecting me, why did you have this man follow us?" Austin asked.

"Man?!" said a girl's voice. The cloaked man took their hood off, and the man was, in fact, a girl. A tan girl with long brown hair and light blue eyes. "Who are you calling a man?" she asked, getting in Austin's face.

"Now, now, Mona. I'm sure he didn't know you were a girl," the man said.

"Yeah, I'm really sorry, Mona." he said, looking at the old man and back at the girl. "I didn't mean to upset you. I just- why did you follow and spy and us?" Austin asked.

"Because I asked her too," the old man said.

"I had to make sure you were the one," Mona said.

"The one?" Austin asked.

"I want to show you something." the old man said.

There was a small cave under the waterfall. There were cave paintings all around.

"It reads, *'the Light of the Sun will cast away the darkest shadow'*," Mona said, looking at the cave painting.

"What does it mean?" Austin asked.

"I believe it's referring to you, Austin." the old man said.

"Me?" Austin asked.

"For the longest time we believed the sun light was the answer. That's why the Egyptians worshiped Ra, the Sun God. Recently, I haven't been so sure. Yin is the light. You are his son. You are the Son of Light," the old man said, looking at Austin and Yin. "You are the light that will cast away the shadows."

"So what or who are the shadows?" Austin asked.

"The Gods… If the Gods are the shadows, that means Yang is the darkest one," Yin said.

"Right you are," the old man said, "If you look for the light, you will eventually find it. If you look for darkness, that is all you will ever see. Austin, you are the light the world has been looking for," the old man said.

"That is a lot to live up to. It's a lot of responsibility for one kid," Austin said.

A God Among Men

"You have help," Yin said, putting his arm around Austin. "I will be with you every step of the way. I may not remember everything, but I will always help."

"Thank you," Austin said, looking up at Yin.

The old man started to walk out of the cave. "Mona, you will also help, correct?"

"Me?" Mona asked.

"Yes, you. I figured you wouldn't mind after I overheard you say Austin was cute," the old man said with a little laugh.

Austin blushed and turned back to look at Mona. Mona stood there making a fist by her side, blushing and shy that the old man said that.

They were on their way back to Olivia, Marcus, and Mr. Kale.

"Excuse me, sir. How do you know what's going on out in the world? The people here act as if they have never seen someone from outside before," Austin asked.

"I know a lot of things, young man. I've been around awhile," the old man said.

"Do you think you could help us? We're looking for something that could help us in our fight. A sword," Austin said.

"A sword?" Mona asked.

Austin turned to look back at her. "Yes, it's a weapon that has the power to kill a God. It looks like a raven feather," Austin said.

"A sword that looks like a raven feather?" There was a slight pause "Ah yes, I have seen something like that before," the old man said.

"You have? Do you know where it is?" Austin asked in excitement.

"Of course I know where it is. It's mine," he said.

"Yours?... wait... are you, Aggon?" Austin asked with a confused look on his face. He looked up at Yin. Yin slowly turned back to look at the man. "Are you?"

"It is good to see you, my old friend," Aggon said with a tear in his eye as he gave Yin a hug. It had been a very long time since he had seen his friend.

"But how? You were alive with the First Men. That was thousands of years ago," Austin asked.

"Like I said. I've been around for a while. Yin maybe the God of Light, but he is also the God of Life. Before he lost his memory, he blessed me with a long and wonderful life." Aggon put his arm on Austin's shoulder and took his walking stick and pointed it all around. "Austin, this is the city of the First Men. After the humans rebelled and the Gods started destroying everything, Yin got my family and me out of Egypt. We ended up settling down here. Yin helped build this place for us. He kept it hidden from the other Gods. Once he lost his memory, he forgot who we were and where we were." He turned to Yin, "And I do not blame you at all, my friend."

"I am so sorry, Aggon," Yin said. "I have let a lot of people down."

"Don't worry, Yin, we will make everything right," Austin added.

"I do not doubt that at all," Aggon said.

"Aggon, if you don't mind me asking, how were you able to survive down here? I mean, your friend forgot about all this and you. He could have provided for you but wasn't here. It was just you and your family," Austin asked.

"That is a good question, Austin. I will admit I was at my lowest. Things were not looking good. I was struggling to provide for my family. But let me give you these words of advice. When we hit our lowest points, we are open to the greatest change." Aggon turned to look at the city and the people working in it. "That's exactly what we did. We changed. My family decided to help others in need. One by one, we went out into the world and found people and brought them back with us. Mona here was abandoned as a baby. Left in a side ally on a rainy night. We found her and brought her back with us." Aggon turned to look at Austin. "Anything you need to put an end to the God's rule is yours. I will take you to the sword."

Austin looked up at Yin. He couldn't believe it after all this time. They were about to have what they had been searching for.

Austin and Yin made it back to Olivia, Marcus, and Mr. Kale. They were sitting under the stone pavilion with a hot meal in front of them. "Hey, guys, what's going on?" Austin asked.

"I guess being friends with the God of Light and the Son of Light has its perks," Marcus said.

"Well, there are two people I want you to meet." Austin turned and held his hand out, "This is Mona. She was the one that was following us, wearing the cloak. She will also be helping us."

Olivia didn't like the way Mona was looking at Austin.

"And this," there was a pause. "This is Aggon." Marcus spit the food right out of his mouth, "Like the old dude from history class? The dude with the sword?"

"Yes, friend of Austin's. That is me," Aggon said. "Now, my friends. You have had a long journey. Please eat. I will have people draw up baths for each of you. I will take you to the sword soon enough."

Chapter 17
Eye Of The Storm

Olivia was in her bath, bubbles all around and steam in the air. She had her eyes closed, and she was relaxing. She heard a noise and quickly opened her eyes. She looked around the room, but no one was there. She took a deep breath, laid back in the bath and closed her eyes again. She heard the noise again and once again looked around the room. This time she saw Mona sitting in the window.

"Hello," Mona said in a little flirty voice.

"Hi?" Olivia said. "Can I help you?"

Mona got down from the window. "No. So your Austin's girlfriend?" Mona asked.

"Well, we didn't make it official, why did he say something?" Olivia asked.

Mona walked to the door smiling. "Nope, I was just wondering. Better get dressed. Everyone is waiting."

Mona left the room. Olivia grabbed her towel. She was wondering what that was all about.

Olivia met everyone down at the pavilion. Her hair was still drying. She looked to her left and saw Mona smiling and waving at her. Mona then waved to Austin. Austin waved back. Olivia gave Mona an angry look.

"Hey, you okay?" Austin asked.

Olivia turned, "Yeah, I'm okay. It was a very nice bath. That was very nice of them." She reached and grabbed Austin's hand.

"Yeah, it was very refreshing," Austin said. He turned to look back toward Aggon. Olivia turned to Mona and winked at her. Mona was not smiling anymore. She looked annoyed.

"Okay. Everyone well fed and well refreshed?" Aggon asked.

"Yes, thank you so much for that," Mr. Kale said.

"Good, good. Everyone follow me," Aggon said as he turned to walk down the steps in a cave behind the pavilion. Everyone followed Aggon. He turned to look at Austin. "Yin helped me make this so no one would find it." About halfway down the tunnel, he put his walking stick in a hole in the wall and turned it.

"It's a key?" Mona asked.

"Of course. I always have it with me, so I won't lose it," Aggon said.

A secret tunnel opened which led them to an empty room.

"There's nothing here," Marcus said.

"Not yet," Aggon replied. He twisted off the top of his walking stick. The top part was another key. There was one more keyhole. This time it was on the ground in the center of the room. Once he turned the key, a hidden latch opened. Aggon opened the hatch, and a gold box arose from the ground.

"Austin, would you like to do the honors?" Aggon asked.

Austin nodded his head and walked forward. He put his hands on the lid and slowly opened it. There, lying in the golden box, was Aggon's Sword. It shined in the light. The weapon they had been searching for and talking about the whole school year was right in front of him. Austin slowly reached for the handle.

"Austin," Aggon said. Austin pulled his hand back and looked up at Aggon.

"Yes?" he asked.

"There is something special about this sword. Only a certain type of person can use it to its full potential. Only the pure of heart will be able to use its true power. To anyone else, it's just a regular sword," Aggon said.

Austin nodded. He slowly reached down to the handle. They all watched closely. He grabbed the handle and lifted the sword over his head. They all waited for something to happen... but nothing did. Austin lowered his arm and looked at Aggon.

"How do I know if it worked?" Austin's asked. Aggon seemed disappointed that nothing had happened. "The sword will shine as bright as a star," Aggon said.

Austin looked down at the sword. It just looked like a regular blade in the shape of a feather. Everyone stood there in silence for a little bit. The sword didn't shine bright at all. Austin was getting angry. "This was the only thing that could stop The Storm. And it doesn't even work." They all were disappointed.

Marcus's face lit up. "No, but maybe it doesn't need to!" he said in excitement.

"What are you talking about?" Mr. Kale asked.

"Just hear me out. The Storm thinks the sword was destroyed, right? Maybe he doesn't know that it shines bright when at full power. If Austin shows up with the sword, maybe he will think he doesn't have a chance. Maybe he will not want to die and agree to leave Earth?" Marcus suggested.

"That's actually not a bad idea," Olivia said.

"How do I become pure of heart?" Austin asked Aggon.

"It's not something I can help you with. The Sword decides for itself if you are pure of heart," Aggon said.

They left the cave and were back at the pavilion. Men and women from the city were bringing supplies for them for the rest of their trip.

"You all have a very important task ahead of you. We wanted to make sure you had everything you needed before you left. The world will be a better place soon," Aggon said as the group packed their bags.

"Don't be strangers if you are ever in the area." Aggon shook Austin's hand, "May we meet again."

They waved to everyone as they walked back up to the entrance of the Lost City. Austin made sure to grab the coin he had left in the raven's eye. Once they got outside, they started loading the car.

"Austin!" said a voice from inside the giant doorway. They all turned around and saw Mona running toward them. "Did you think you could get rid of me that fast? I'm coming to help!"

Olivia just rolled her eyes. Austin smiled and thanked her. "Yin and I will keep you safe."

"Don't worry about me. I can take care of myself," she said as she put her pack in the car. They all climbed in.

"Do we know where we are going?" Marcus asked. Olivia pulled out her phone. "That very big hurricane is over an island off the coast of Norway."

"An island? What would he be doing there?" Austin asked.

"Maybe he doesn't want his home destroyed? Battle on neutral ground?" Marcus asked.

"I don't think The Storm would try and make it a fair fight," Olivia said.

"He may have his reasons," Austin's dad said. He called his pilot friend and made arrangements for a private plane to the island. They got to the airport and waited until the plane was ready. The flight was a couple of hours, so they would be able to get their rest. All except Austin, as he was anticipating coming face to face with The Storm again.

Once they landed, Mr. Kale woke everyone up. Yin was on the outside of the plane, guiding them through the hurricane.

Olivia checked her phone again, and the hurricane tripled in size. "He must know we're here," she said.

"Let's hope our plan works," Austin said. They all grabbed their bags. Austin had the sword in hand, ready to confront The Storm. The rain and wind were crazy the moment they stepped off the plane. They had to walk with their arms up, blocking the wind and rain from their faces.

"Where do we even go?" Olivia said loudly for everyone to hear.

"The eye of the hurricane is the calmest spot. Let's head there and start looking," Austin's dad said.

The group started following Olivia's weather app to get to the eye of the hurricane. Lighting was striking all around them. Tornados, we're touching down, ripping up trees and rocks. It didn't look like there were any houses or people nearby, just a big grassy plain with trees and large rocks and a cliff to their left that led to the ocean. Yin had to jump in front of the group a few times to block flying trees from hitting the group. One large tree was flying right toward them. Yin clapped his hands together. Just as the tree hit his fingertips, it split in half. Each half flew past both sides of the group. After navigating through one of the worst hurricanes in history, they came to a clearing. The winds died down, and the heavy rain turned into a light drizzle. Everything around them was more visible. They all looked up.

"We made it to the eye of the hurricane," Marcus said.

"Now what?" Mona asked.

"We need to find The Storm," Austin said.

"Or he's going to find us," Olivia said, pointing across the grassy field they were standing on. There was a group of The Storm's men standing in a line. Behind them... was The Storm.

Austin took his pack off and started to take a few steps forward. "Yin," he said.

"Right behind you," Yin said as he also stepped forward.

"I knew you would be foolish enough to come to me," The Storm said. His voice rolled with the thunder.

"You have something I want. And I'm not leaving until I get her back!" Austin yelled.

"Oh, you mean her?" The Storm said, holding up the cage Elsie was in.

"Elsie," Austin said to himself. "Let her go, and I will spare you."

"Spare me?" The Storm tossed the cage to the side like it was trash. Elsie tumbled inside until the cage came to a stop. "Don't make me laugh," The Storm yelled back to Austin.

"You won't be laughing for too long," Austin said as he held up the Sword of Aggon.

"What is that?! It was supposed to be destroyed," Storm yelled with slight fear in his voice.

"I guess your queen doesn't know all she thinks she does," Austin said.

"Watch your mouth, boy," The Storm said as he pointed over at Austin and the group.

Loud thunder crashed, and lighting was striking everywhere. The Storm's men ran toward them. The Storm held his hand up and closed it to make a fist. The eye of the hurricane closed. The rain and the wind started to pick back up.

"I guess this is it," Austin gripped the sword tight and held it close. Olivia, Marcus, Mona, and Mr. Kale ran back for cover behind a large rock. Austin's dad pulled out a large knife from his bag.

"Just in case," he said as Olivia, Marcus, and Mona just looked at him with worry on their faces.

Austin and Yin stood ready. The Storm's huntsmen outnumbered their whole group. It was going to be a lot of work for Austin and Yin to make sure they don't get to the others. Austin, of course, used the sword to cut a few of the huntsmen down. Yin was able to launch a large rock into a few of the huntsmen, adding a few blasts of light energy.

"I hope everything is going okay out there," Olivia said.

A few of the huntsmen got past Austin and Yin. Two jumped out around the rock they were hiding behind, one on each side. Mona quickly grabbed the knife from Austin's dad's hand. She threw it across her body and struck a huntsman right in the chest. She got up very quickly and turned and jumped off the rock toward the other huntsman. She wrapped her legs around his head and flipped him over. She grabbed a smaller rock and hit him on the side of the head. She looked up and saw a third huntsman had come around and grabbed Olivia. Mona looked down and grabbed a small knife from the belt of the man she was kneeling over. She quickly threw it at the third huntsmen. Olivia was let go. She got back over to Marcus and Mr. Kale and looked up at the third huntsman. The knife was sticking out of his neck. He fell straight back.

"I'm sticking with her," Marcus said after watching her take down three grown men in less than a minute.

Austin's dad grabbed the knife from the man's chest. "Maybe you should hold on to this," he said, handing it to Mona.

They all peeked their heads out to see the last huntsman fall to the sword in Austin's hand. Suddenly, a lightning bolt struck Austin in the shoulder, knocking him down. Olivia, Marcus, and Austin's dad all screamed for Austin. Seeing him get hit like that was a shock to them.

"Austin!" Yin yelled as he ran to him. He helped Austin get up. "Get to cover. Let me handle him."

"You aren't strong enough," Austin said as he tried to catch his breath. "You don't have your full power."

"It's not always about how strong you are, but about how you use what you have," Yin said back to Austin.

A God Among Men

The lightning hit Austin hard and hurt him a lot. Austin got back to his feet, holding his shoulder.

"Aww, did I hurt you?" The Storm asked.

Austin ran back to the rest of the group. Olivia and his dad looked at Austin to make sure he was okay. Slight touches to his shoulder caused pain.

Storm and Yin stood facing each other, staring each other down. Austin and the group watched on as a battle of cosmic forces were about to collide. Storm struck first before any words could be spoken between the two of them. He started sending bolts of lightning toward Yin. Yin was ready, deflecting them with a shield of pure light energy he made by holding both his hand out in front of him.

Yin retaliated with a barrage of light energy blasts. Each one struck Storm with powerful force. Storm was furious, throwing lightning bolt after lightning bolt. Yin was quick on his feet, dodging each one as they came toward him. This made Storm even more angry. He made lightning fall from the skies. Still throwing lightning bolts at Yin. Yin was trying to tire out Storm. Yin hadn't attacked since the beginning of the fight.

Yin saw Storm becoming tired. Yin shot a blast of light energy out from his hand. Storm shot a blast of continuous lightning from his hand. The two blasts collided with each other, neither one giving in to the other. Yin shot a ball of light energy out from his other hand at The Storm's foot. As soon as it hit, Storm fell to one knee. Yin stopped his first blast. He spun out of the way of The Storms blast and glided quickly right toward The Storm. He was hoping to give a final blow.

Right as Yin was within reach, The Storm grabbed Yin by the neck. The Storm looked very angry. His eyes were glowing light blue. Austin saw this and was now scared for Yin. The Storm's hand had electricity surrounding it, electrocuting Yin. The storm stood up, lifting Yin off the ground. He was squeezing his hand around Yin's neck. Yin screamed in pain. Both of his hands were trying to loosen the grip The Storm had on him. Nothing was working. Yin took one of his hands and grabbed The Storms face. Yin's hand started to glow white. A blast of light energy came from his hand from point blank range onto The Storm's face. This caused The Storm to fly backward and Yin in the opposite direction.

The Storm lifted his head as he was holding his face. He stood up, and with all his anger, he shot more bolts of lightning at Yin. Yin jumped out of the way one more time. Only this time, The Storm anticipated it, and as soon as Yin's foot touched the ground, lighting struck his foot. This caused Yin to be unbalanced. Storm threw one final lightning bolt and knocked Yin back. Storm smiled because now he had Yin right where he wanted him. Storm raised his hand up and threw it down, bringing a large lightning strike from the sky which landed a devastating strike on Yin. Storm held his hand in front of him and pulled it back to him fast while making a fist. A lightning bolt came from behind Yin.

"Yin, look out!" Austin yelled.
Yin turned around just as the bolt struck him in the shoulder. Austin looked on as Yin's body lay still, his body charred and smoking.

Storm just laughed, "I didn't think it would be this easy to defeat the all-powerful God of Light."

A God Among Men

Austin reached down and grabbed the sword, "Let's end this." He started to take a few steps toward The Storm, which turned into a run. Austin jumped into the air holding the sword over his head. He was about to slam the sword right into The Storm's back as The Storm turned around and caught the sword. Austin just looked shocked.

"How sad. You should never try and trick a God," The Storm said. He punched Austin, forcing him to let go of the sword. Austin dropped to the ground. This time, he was holding his side when The Storm hit him. The Storm threw the sword away from Austin.

A ball of light energy came out of nowhere and knocked The Storm to the ground. He turned to look and saw Yin slowly standing up.

"I've had enough of you!" The Storm yelled. He stood up and raised his hand in the air. Lightning came down right on top of Yin, but Yin was able to redirect it. Yin turned back to look at The Storm only to get hit by another bolt thrown by him. Yin fell to the ground.

"You are a weak old man!" The Storm yelled. Austin saw this and needed to get the attention back on him.

"So," he said as he slowly got back to his feet. The Storm turned to Austin. "Are you like, supposed to be Thor?" Austin asked.

This angered The Storm. "Does it look like I need a damn hammer?!" he yelled. He held his hands up in the air, and lighting struck all around at the same time. The Storm got close to Austin and punched him in the gut. Electricity surrounded his fist, launching Austin into the air. He landed back on the ground hard.

Olivia ran out to Austin, "Austin, please get up."

He could hardly stand but was able to get back to his feet.

"You guys need to get to Elsie and get her free. We will take care of The Storm," he said to Olivia.

"Okay," she said as she ran back to the others. Austin was able to get behind a different rock.

The Storm kept throwing lightning at the rock he was behind. "Come out here, Austin. I want everyone to watch when I kill you!" The Storm yelled.

"He's too strong," Austin said to himself as he looked over at Yin. Yin looked at Austin and nodded. Austin nodded back.

Austin took a deep breath, got up, and ran out from behind the rock. Austin was trying to keep The Storm's back toward Elsie. Everyone else was able to sneak from rock to rock to tree to get to Elsie.

"Dad!" Elsie said with tears in her eyes. She was so happy to see her dad.

"Hi, sweetie," he said, crying also.

"Don't worry. We will get you out of this cage soon," Marcus said.

He grabbed a rock and started slamming it onto the lock to try and break it. Austin got right in front of The Storm and threw a punch. This time it was able to stagger The Storm.

The Storm grabbed his jaw. "I see you've gotten stronger." The Storm quickly hit back, slamming Austin into the ground. Austin could barely get back to his feet. The Storm grabbed Austin by his head and lifted him up. Austin screamed in pain. Yin used all the strength he could. He stood up and held his hands out in front of him. He shot a beam of light energy that struck Storm hard before Yin fell.

A God Among Men

The Storm dropped Austin back on the ground. The Storm was very angry. He kicked Austin in the chest, just like at prom. Austin flew back, his body skipped on the ground and crashed into tree. Austin could not move. His body was too weak to keep going. He debated on just lying there and giving up. It took all his strength to turn his head to see his friends and his dad trying to rescue Elsie. He remembered he had something to fight for. He used all his strength to get back up. He fell back down a few times but was able to get back to his feet.

"Storm!" Austin yelled.

"When will you learn?" The Storm said back. Olivia turned to look. She watched as Austin and The Storm ran at each other. The Storm's eyes lit up blue. His fist started glowing also. Austin was running at full speed. To Olivia's amazement, she thought she saw Austin's fist glow white. They both punched, their fists colliding with each other, causing an explosion. Olivia watched as Austin and The Storm both flew backward onto the ground. The storm was able to get up and see that Olivia, Marcus, Mona, and Austin's dad were trying to break Elsie free.

"You dare try and free my prisoner?!" The Storm yelled.

Austin's dad saw him and stood up in front of Olivia, Marcus, Mona, and Elsie with his arms out. "You will not harm any of my kids!" Austin's dad yelled.

The Storm made a lightning bolt in his hand. Austin saw this and quickly ran to get in front of his dad. Yin lifted his head to see what was happening. The Storm threw the lightning bolt. Austin ran as fast as he could. He leaped into the air reaching his hand out as far as he could. All he needed to do was make the lightning hit him instead of his dad. His hand was so close. Austin passed in front of his dad in the air. He rolled on the ground and quickly looked up. His whole world stopped. His dad crashed to the ground. Austin watched as his dad just laid there, not moving.

"Dad?" Austin's said as tears ran down his face. "Dad, get up!" Austin crawled toward his dad and rolled him over. There was a burn mark on his shirt and chest from where the lightning struck. Olivia, Marcus, and Mona just watch as Austin cried over his dad's body.

Marcus, in anger, slammed the rock on the lock one more time and finally breaks it off. Elsie was able to crawl to her dad, also. Elsie put her head on her dad's chest.

"Daddy, please come back to me. I just got back to you," she said through her tears.

"What a lovely family reunion. Maybe we should pay mommy and baby sister a visit also," The Storm said.

Austin stood up. His head was down. Blood mixed with tears and rain dripping from his face. Cuts and bruises covered his body through his ripped shirt. He started walking toward The Storm.

"Ready to die? You can be with your stupid father again. Did he really think he could stop me?" The Storm asked.

Austin ran straight for Storm, and with all his anger, he jumped into the air and punched The Storm. The Storm punched back. They were trading punch for punch. The Storm was able to outlast Austin. Austin punched and missed, and The Storm hit him with the back of his fist. Austin once again flew back and crashed onto the ground. He thought he was dead. He couldn't feel any part of his body anymore. Yin started to stand up.

"Not a chance. You are not interfering anymore," The Storm yelled as he threw a lightning bolt at Yin. Yin crashed onto the ground near Austin. Yin was not as strong as he used to be ever since he stopped Yang from coming to Earth.

The Storm turned to the rest of the group. "Who's next?" he asked.

"Is... that... all you... got?"

The Storm turned back to see Austin standing there, wobbling with his fists up.

"Enough of this guy!" The Storm yelled as he held his hand up, and lightning struck Austin. Austin dropped where he stood, Not moving, not breathing.

"No!!" Olivia screamed in pain and sadness. She tried getting up to run to Austin, but Marcus was holding her back.

"Olivia, no! It's too late! He's gone!" he said through his tears.

Mona fell to her knees. Tears rolled down her face, "It's over. We lost. We failed."

Olivia hung her head low. She crawled to Elsie. Elsie could barely breathe. For a second, she had her dad and big brother back, and now they are both gone for good. She and Olivia cried. Yin lifted his head to see Austin lying there.

"Big brother, please come back. I need you!" Elsie screamed.

"Austin, please get up!" Olivia screamed. "Austin, I love you! Please!" You could hear the pain in everyone's voice. Austin's body was lying there lifeless. No sign of movement at all.

The Storm laughed, "Don't worry, you two can share a cage after we go home." The Storm went back to laughing.

When we hit our lowest point, we are open to the greatest change.

That's all Austin could hear in his head. Austin's eyes opened and were glowing the brightest white. Austin's body lifted off the ground.

"Storm!" Austin said with Yin's voice echoing behind his. It echoed all throughout the sky. The Storm stopped laughing and turned to see Austin flying there, alive.

"No! That's impossible! I watched you die!" The Storm said in disbelief.

"Storm. You have been terrorizing this Earth and the people on it long enough. It's time you meet your permanent end!" Austin's echoey voice filled the air. Olivia, Elsie, Marcus, and Mona couldn't believe what they were seeing. Yin couldn't believe it either. Was that really Austin? How did he survive?

Elsie looked and saw Aggon's sword. She started crawling toward it. The Storm made a lightning bolt in his hand and threw it at Austin. Austin caught it right next to his head and shot his other hand out, causing a big, white beam to blast out of his hand. It hit The Storm, forcing his body to skip on the ground, crashing into trees and rocks behind him. He finally came to a stop and began to stand up but was met by Austin's fist only to be slammed backed into the ground. Austin picked Storm up by his neck and used his other hand to punch him back to where the fight started.

A God Among Men

The Storm crashed into the ground again. He struggled to get up, "Please have mercy!" he begged.

"Sorry, it's too late for that." Austin's echoey voice said.

Austin grabbed The Storm's leg and flew straight up in the air. Once, they were a few hundred yards in the sky. The Storm tried making lightning strike Austin. That had no effect on him. With The Storm still hanging by his leg, Austin looked down at him. He let his hand go as The Storm began to fall. Austin shot a blast of light energy down at The Storm which forced him to fall faster and harder. Austin flew straight down cutting through his own blast. Right before The Storm hit the ground, Austin caught up with him, put his feet on his chest, and slammed him into the ground. This caused a large crater to form.

Elsie was able to get to the sword. She grabbed it and picked it up. The sword began shining as bright as a star.

Olivia saw this and gasped, "A pure heart!"

Austin saw this with his glowing eyes. He picked up The Storm. Shot his hand out again. A beam of white light shot out, blasting The Storm back again. Crashing into the ground right in front of Elsie. The Storm slowly turned his head to see Elsie with the sword.

"This is for my dad." Elsie took the sword and raised it high and drove it right into the chest of The Storm. The Storms screamed, and eyes lit up blue but slowly faded away. Now The Storm just laid there lifeless with the sword sticking from his chest. Austin flew back into the air. He looked up at the sky and held his hand up high. The hurricane began to fade. The winds died down. The rain stopped. Tornadoes disappeared, and the sun began to shine bright on the world once again.

Chapter 18
The Unexpected

Austin's eyes slowly went back to normal as he floated back down to the ground. Once his feet touched down, Austin passed out and fell to the ground. His body had never taken a beating like that in his whole life. Yin crawled over to Austin and put his hand on Austin's shoulder. Yin's eyes turned white, and Austin took a deep breath and opened his eyes. Austin sat up slowly. They were able to help each other up but Austin did not seem fully healed.

"What happened?" Austin asked.

"You did it. You won," Yin said as he looked around. All he could see was destruction. Trees were knocked over, rocks moved and the ground was torn up. Huntsmen laid everywhere. It truly looked like a battleground.

"We didn't win," Austin said as he looked over at Elsie leaning over their dad. Yin looked down at Austin and then over at Elsie. "The war has just begun," Austin said. He slowly walked over to his sister and dad.

Yin just watched him. He could feel Austin's sadness. Yin turned and looked up at the sky. He knew Yang was watching and that this was far from over.

Olivia met Austin halfway. She gave him a big hug and still couldn't believe he was alive.

"I thought I lost you," Olivia said.

Austin didn't say a word. He just kept walking. Olivia didn't blame him. She wished there was some way she could help him. He fell to his knees right next to Elsie. She turned and gave him a big hug. The only sound in the air was the sound of Elsie and Austin crying over their dad. Olivia and Marcus were trying to hold back the tears. It was too hard since Mr. Kale was a second dad to them. Mona was sitting on a rock. She shed a few tears as she could feel the sadness in the air. She looked at Yin and decided to walk over toward him.

"So now what?" Mona asked Yin.

"Now we go home." Yin turned to look at Mr. Kale lying there. "All of us."

Yin was able to make it back to the plane. He explained everything to the pilot. The pilot was in shock after he heard the news. He remembered that he made a promise to Mr. Kale before they took off that no matter what, he needed to get the kids home. The pilot got the emergency stretcher out and followed Yin to the rest of the group. Yin and the pilot were carrying Austin's dad on the stretcher back to the plane.

Once they were back to the plane, they all got on except Austin, he was standing on the edge of the cliff staring out into the horizon. Olivia looked out of the plane and saw him standing there. She got off the plane and walked over to him.

A God Among Men

"Hey, Austin? The plane is almost ready. Take all the time you need." Olivia turned to walk back to the plane.

"I love you," Austin said.
Olivia froze and turned around.

"What did you say?" she asked.

"You said it first," Austin turned to look at Olivia. She just smiled at him and blushed. They hugged for a little while. Austin then looked Olivia in the eyes and kissed her.

"I don't know why it took me this long to kiss you," Austin said.

"Don't stop now," Olivia said back, and they kissed again.

"You guys are adorable." They both turned to see Marcus standing there watching them. "The planes ready. Sorry I didn't want to interrupt," Marcus added, then he turned to walk to the plane. Austin's and Olivia smiled at each other and turned to get on the plane as well.

The plane ride was a long and quiet one. Austin made sure Elsie was okay and that she had enough water and food. He helped bandage her up. He made sure she had ice for whatever hurt. "Get some rest. You are safe now," Austin said. Elsie smiled and fell asleep on Austin's shoulder.

Back home, Austin's mom was waiting for the plane to land. She couldn't wait to see her husband, Austin, and Elsie again. She held her hand up to block the sunlight. She could see the plane about to land. Ava was back home with their grandmother. She was visiting in town and offered to stay and watch Ava while Mrs. Kale picked everyone up.

Mrs. Kale was standing at the gate watching the plane come to a stop. When the door opened, she watched as Olivia, Marcus, Yin, and a girl she didn't know all exited the plane. She watched closely as Austin slowly got to the top of the steps. Everyone turned to make sure he got down the stairs okay. Austin turned his head and held his arm out. Elsie walked to him, and they put their arms around each other, helping each other down the stairs.

Their mom started crying because she was so happy to see her little girl again. She ran over to them and gave Austin and Elsie a big hug and kissed them on the cheeks. "I missed you both and your father so much," their mom said.

Austin and Elsie looked at each other. Tears began to form in their eyes. Their mom looked up at the top of the stairs. "Where is your father? Shouldn't he have gotten off by now?" She looked back down at Austin and Elsie. Austin shut his eyes tight, trying to fight the tears. He just shook his head.

"He..." Elsie was also trying to fight it. "He saved us, mom. He protected us."

Their mom started to cry "Is he...?" She couldn't finish that sentence. She didn't want to. They all knew what she was going to ask. Elsie couldn't fight it any longer. She burst into tears and hugged her mom tight. Elsie nodded her head to answer her mom's question. Their mom looked up at Austin and could see he wasn't able to fight it either. She grabbed him and pulled him close. They all stood there crying. Everyone else hung their head. They didn't know what to do or say. Olivia walked to them and joined the hug. Marcus followed. They wanted to let Austin, Elsie, and their mom know that they were there for them. That they will always be there for them.

A week went by, and it was not like any normal week. Things moved slower in the Kale house. Elsie had trouble sleeping in her bed. Every night she woke up screaming. Mona shared her room since she had nowhere else to stay. Austin's mom was more than happy to let her stay with them. Mona was able to get up quickly to help Elsie back to sleep before waking Ava. Austin didn't get much sleep those nights either. He would stay awake in his bed hearing Elsie scream each night. He blamed himself even though no one else did.

One Saturday morning, they all woke up and ate breakfast together for the first time since coming home. No one said a word. This wasn't just a normal Saturday. Austin put on his best suit. Elsie put on a nice dress and then let Mona wear one of hers since they were about the same size. Ava had a baby dress on, and their mom also had one on as well. They all met at the front door. Once they opened it, Marcus, Olivia, her parents, and Yin were all waiting outside. They were also in suits and dresses. They were on their way to Mr. Davidson's and Mr. Kale's funerals. They all got in their cars and started to drive toward the funeral home.

"Your dad's pilot friend made a few calls to his and your dad's friends from the military," Olivia said to everyone in the car.

As they were driving, they saw the whole town and military personnel standing on the sides of the roads. People made signs that read:

We will miss you, Mr. Kale. We will miss you, Mr. Davidson. You will not be forgotten. Thank you for everything.

The military had a giant flag hanging over the road as they drove underneath it with the caskets. Mr. Davidson was a teacher that everyone had if they went to Silverdale High School. Austin's dad was someone who always helped out in the community and served in the military before Austin was born. No matter what, they both put others before themselves and would always lend a helping hand. They decided to hold a combined funeral for both of them. It was getting to the end of the funeral.

"Austin?" a voice said. Austin must have been hearing things.

"Austin? Do you want to say a few words?" the voice said again.

Olivia nudged Austin's arm. He looked over at her, and she raised her eyebrows as if she was trying to point to something. Austin looked up to see the pastor looking at him.

"Austin, would you like to come to say a few words?" the pastor asked.

Austin stood up and walked to the podium. "My dad…" there was a pause. "Mr. Davidson was more than a teacher. He was my friend, and I…" there was another pause. Austin looked at both caskets for a while. "They were the bravest men I knew," Austin could only think about all the help Mr. Davidson gave him and the fact he dropped everything to go with them on their trip. He also pictured his dad standing there protecting Olivia, Marcus, Mona, and Elsie.

"I love you, dad. I will miss you so much," Austin said before he had to walk away.

After the funeral, they all went back to Austin's house. Austin, Marcus, and Olivia were sitting on the couch. Austin's mom and Olivia's parents were talking in the living room. Elsie and Mona were sitting on the steps. They heard a loud pounding on the front door. Austin's mom went and opened the front door.

There were a few men in suits and ties standing out front.

"Can I help you?" Austin's mom asked.

"Hello, ma'am. I'm special agent Watson. I'm with the FBI. We're looking for Austin Kale. Is he home?" the man said, holding up his FBI badge and ID. Mrs. Kale turned and looked at Austin. He stood up from the couch. They were all confused. They all just looked at the men walking into their home. They walked in front of Austin. "Austin Kale. You are under arrest for the murders of Evan Turner, Cooper Davidson, and Brian Kale."

"Excuse me?" Austin asked.

"There has to be some kind of mistake!" Austin's mom said as she was trying to talk to the agents. They spun Austin around and put handcuffs on him.

"Wait, who is Evan Turner?" Olivia asked.

One of the agents pulled out his phone and showed a video. This video was taken back at the beginning of the school year. It was the video that showed Austin fighting the people picking on Elsie outside school. Austin shoved his hand forward, and the thug, who must be Evan Turner, was pushed back and smacked into a car parked on the other side of the road. Breaking his back and neck, killing him instantly. No one knew what to say about that.

Everyone looked scared and concerned. The agents took Austin out of the house.

"Austin, don't say anything until we get our lawyer!" his mom yelled out the door.

They put him in the back of the police car. Leaving everyone confused about what just happened inside the house. Once the police left, Austin's mom fainted. Marcus caught her. This had been too much on Austin's mom. First she lost Elsie and now getting her back. Then lost her husband, and now her son was taken from her. Austin, sat in the back of the police car, turned around to watch his home get smaller and smaller as he was driven away. Wondering what will happen next.

End of Book 1

A God Among Men

In New York City. A light blue 1967 mustang pulled up in front of a large building. The door opened. A woman stepped out. She was wearing light blue heels, and a large, heavy blue jacket. Her eyes were crystal blue, like a sapphire. She had long light blue hair. "So, this is the Earth?" she asked as a snowstorm formed behind her.